Mom for Mayor

Mom for Mayor

Nancy Edwards

Illustrated by
Michael Chesworth

Cricket Books
Chicago

Library of Congress Cataloging-in-Publication data

Edwards, Nancy, 1952-
Mom for mayor / by Nancy Edwards ; illustrated by
Michael Chesworth. — 1st ed.
        p. cm.
Summary: Upon learning that the city has sold his neighbor-
hood park to developers, fifth-grader Eric Clark determines
to help his community by getting his mother elected mayor.
ISBN-13: 978-0-8126-2743-5
ISBN-10: 0-8126-2743-1

[1. Elections--Fiction. 2. Mayors--Fiction. 3. Parks--Fiction.
4. Family life--Fiction. 5. Schools--Fiction.] I. Chesworth,
Michael, ill. II. Title.
PZ7.E2633Mom 2006
[Fic]--dc22

                                    2005025412

For Ann, my mentor, my friend
—NE

For Harrison Gregg, Moderator
—MC

Many thanks are due to these people from my community who took the time to share their expertise:

Laurie Sample-Wynn, former mayor

Pauline Repp and Sue Child, City Clerk and Deputy City Clerk

Robert Clegg, City Engineer

If any errors remain, they are mine and mine alone.

A special thanks goes to my editor, Paula Morrow, for her amazing ability to ask just the right questions.

Table of Contents

Mom for Mayor

Chapter 1
Lenox Field

Run! The word pounded in my brain, my heart pounded in my chest, and my breath came out in little white puffs as I raced through the woods. Fast as I was going, I still had to watch where I stepped. March in Michigan turns packed-down trails to mush.

I looked behind me. So far so good. They hadn't caught up to me yet. A few more steps and I'd be free. I ducked under a branch and stepped out into the morning light. A swing set stood in front of me. I grabbed one swing by its chains and leaped over it. I raced to the slide beyond, climbed the ladder, flew down, and landed just steps away from my best friend, Jonathan.

"I made it," I panted.

Jon looked at me and shook his head. "I'll never understand why you insist on taking the

1

long way to the bus stop every day through the woods, over the swings, down the slide." He put his hands on my shoulders and looked me in the eye. "Eric," he said, "you need help."

I grinned at him. "It's easier to avoid space aliens that way," I said. "If I had walked straight down the sidewalk from my house, I could be on my way to Neptune by now."

"Space aliens?" Jon said. "Wasn't it Russian spies yesterday?"

The morning sun reflected off his glasses, giving him a dangerous air. He looked a little like a Russian spy himself. I took off my backpack and set it on the sidewalk.

"Jonathan," I said, and now it was my turn to shake my head. "Despite the fact that you are the smartest kid in our whole fifth-grade class, you just don't have much imagination."

Jon laughed. "That's why I hang out with you. You have enough for both of us."

I turned back and looked again at the woods, the swing, the slide, and the few other pieces of play equipment that lined the side of a baseball field. Lenox Field. As familiar to me as my own bedroom.

I tried to explain. "Lenox Field is just . . ." I stopped and started again. "Walking down the sidewalk I'm Eric Clark, an ordinary fifth grader. But here in Lenox Field, I'm . . . I'm . . ."

I looked over Jon's shoulder and saw the big, new sign.

"For Sale!" I said.

Jon looked at me in surprise. "You're for sale?" he asked.

"Not me," I shouted. "The park! My park!" I stood there staring at the sign. Why would somebody want to buy a park—this park? They sure couldn't be interested in it for the equipment. Judging from the layers of paint on the swings and slide, I figured Lenox Field had been here since the dawn of time, or at least since before I was born. No, if somebody bought this park, I had a pretty strong hunch they weren't planning to share it with me.

"They can't do this to me!" I looked at Jon. "Our baseball games!" I said. "Soccer practice! Kite flying!"

By now a few more people had made their way to our bus stop. I had an audience and I was going to make the most of it. "It's your park, too," I said to them. Amanda Lane, a girl in my class, gave me a worried look, like maybe I was contagious. But the Rossetti twins from first grade looked up at me with respect, and I kept going. "Where else are we going to play? We've got to do something!"

"Like what?" said Amanda.

I looked to Jon for help. Jon always had the answers.

"The park! My park!"

Jon narrowed his eyes as he thought. "The city owns this land," he said. "The mayor wants to sell it and use the money to put up lights at the Greenview Ballpark so they can have night games."

I stared at Jon. "How do you know all this?" I demanded.

He shrugged. "I read it in the newspaper."

"You read the newspaper?" I asked.

"If it has words on it, I read it," he said. "It's a disease or something."

The school bus screeched to a halt, and we climbed on.

"So you knew about this and you didn't even tell me?" I said.

Jon picked a seat by the window. "Why would I?" he asked. "What can a couple of kids do about it, anyway?"

"Do about it!" I exploded, dropping my back-pack on the seat and crowding in next to him. "You just wait and see what we do about it!"

The heater on the bus had been cranked up to "bake." Jon started unzipping his jacket. He stopped mid-zip.

"We?" he said. "As in you and me?" Jon shook his head.

"Of course, you and me. You, the master of knowledge, the guy with the reading disease, the idea man." I paused to let this sink in. Then I humbly touched my chest. "And me, the man of action, unafraid of risk, public opinion . . ."

"Detention."

"We're like Sherlock Holmes and Watson," I argued.

"Right," said Jon. "Or at least Scooby and Shaggy, or Bert and Ernie."

"But you'll help, right?" I asked.

"Help do what?" Jon said, throwing his hands up in the air.

"That's your part," I explained. "You just figure out what to do, and I'll do it."

Jonathan rolled his eyes, slouched down in his seat, and pulled his Red Wings cap down to his glasses. I'd been friends with Jon long enough to know this conversation was finished.

Trees and houses passed by the window. The bus stopped and started as more kids piled on. I kept my mouth shut. I knew if I gave Jonathan enough time, he'd come up with a good idea. I was a patient guy. I was willing to give him all the time in the world. As long as he figured it out before lunch.

Chapter 2

The Traitor

Mrs. Murphy runs our class like a well-oiled machine. She lines us up every morning to hand in our homework as she checks our names off her list. A banner on the wall announces the percent of homework handed in each day. Today it said 94%.

I unzipped my backpack and started searching for my current event. Once a week we have to bring in an article from the newspaper or a magazine and report on it. It's easy homework as long as I remember to do it. I'll cut out an interesting picture the night before and then read about it on its way from my backpack to my desk in the morning. This morning I pulled out February's lunch menu, a broken ruler, some papers with spaceship drawings on them, and an old lunch bag that felt a little squishy.

"Eric?" Mrs. Murphy called.

I made one last desperate dive into my bag. "I cut it out," I said. "I really did. I must have left it on the kitchen table."

Mrs. Murphy wrote my name on the board. There went recess.

My brain was so busy flip-flopping between the double tragedies of No Park and No Recess that I completely missed the first part of Caitlin's current event report. It wasn't until I heard the words "Lenox Field" that I snapped to attention.

"Putting lights around the ball field at Greenview Park means we'll be able to have night games. That means we can have big baseball tournaments here, and that means lots of people coming in from out of town staying and eating and shopping here."

Caitlin has a habit of rocking from side to side when she talks. Her ponytail swayed, and so did my stomach. Greenview Park was on the opposite side of town. It might as well be in a different city.

"My uncle said selling Lenox Field and improving Greenview Park is one of the best ideas he's ever had."

My mouth dropped open. I had known since the second week of school that Caitlin's uncle was the mayor. She worked it into every current event report she possibly could. But until that very moment, it hadn't occurred to me that there was an actual person to blame for selling my park.

I shut my mouth and glared as Caitlin flounced back to her seat. Now I knew who to blame. It was just a matter of time until I figured out what to do about it.

At recess time I had a clear view of the playground from my lonely desk. It was painful. Every swing that sailed through the blue sky, every shriek of laughter was a reminder of the swings at my park, of the laughter that had been mine. And Dad's. Of course Dad hadn't been to the park with me for a long time. But if they sold my park, there'd never be another chance.

I tried to think about what I could do. Chain myself to a slide? Have a Save Our Park parade? Sell cupcakes to raise money to buy the park myself? I sighed. I prayed Jon would have a good idea.

I couldn't talk to Jon at recess because I was stuck inside, and I couldn't talk to him at lunch because he went to Junior Great Books. Computer class was my last chance. We sat side by side in the lab, thirty minutes before the end of the day, and he still hadn't come up with an answer for me. His fingers flew over the keyboard. I rocked my chair back and forth, tapped my foot, and chewed on my pencil. I leaned back too far and had to catch myself from falling.

Now I knew who to blame.

"So what are we going to do?" I asked, replanting all four legs of my chair.

"About what?" Jon said.

"The park, the park, the park!" I said, grabbing my head in both hands. It's not always easy being friends with Jon.

Jon's fingers never missed a beat as they sped through the typing program. "Oh, that," he said. "The answer's on the wall."

I looked around. I saw posters about good keyboard position and a chart of our class's progress through the typing program, but I sure didn't see any answer for the big Park Problem.

"Where?" I asked.

"Back in our room," Jon said. "You really ought to look on the bulletin board once in a while."

I shut my eyes and tried to put the board together piece by piece in my head. I could see big letters cut out of newspaper that said IN THE NEWS surrounded by articles clipped from magazines and newspapers. But where was the answer?

I concentrated. Glossy faces, a volcano somewhere, and maps of Michigan, the USA, and the world. But nowhere, and I was pretty sure about this, was there an article about Lenox Field.

"What is it?" I demanded. I grabbed the mouse away from him. "Unless the answer is dropping Caitlin's uncle into an active volcano, there's absolutely nothing helpful there." The thought made me smile. "Although that does sound like an interesting solution."

Jon stopped typing, took the mouse out of my hand, and looked at me. "Little article," he said. "Upper left-hand corner. No picture, just words."

Jon might love mysteries, but he was driving me crazy. I grabbed his arm. "Help me out here, O brilliant one."

"O.K., then," Jon said with a grin. Then he became serious. "Elections for city council are coming up. The article is about what you have to do to run for city council."

Run for city council? My mind started racing. Run for mayor? Beat out Mr. Park Killer? That would be sweeter than turning him into a lavacicle. "So what do I do?"

Jon gave me a look that could only be pity. He shook his head. "Wait about eight years until you're old enough, that's all," he said. "You can't run for city council. You can't even vote."

"Ah," I said. "But I could be the power behind the throne. I read about that. It's been done. I just need to find the right person. . . ."

I looked up. Three rows ahead, Mrs. Murphy leaned over Justin and Amy's computer. If a ray of sunshine had chosen that moment to fall on her, it couldn't have been any more obvious. Nobody loved government more than Mrs. Murphy. She made us do current events every week. Copies of the Constitution and the Declaration of Independence hung on the wall, along with a big poster of Core Democratic Values.

Even more important, I had a feeling that Mrs. Murphy was tired of hearing about Caitlin's wonderful uncle every single week. Her eyes had a way of drifting off every time Caitlin brought up the subject.

I started working on the perfect words for talking Mrs. Murphy into this. Maybe something like, "Mrs. Murphy, we would learn so much about city government if you would run for city council. . . ."

I was just about to try this out when I heard her voice beside me.

"Eric," she said. There was steel in her voice. This couldn't be good. "Every week you accomplish more talking than typing. Next week I'm putting you with a new partner."

I slid down in my chair. Stupid, stupid, stupid, I thought. How could I ever have believed I could be the power behind *her* throne? I was just lucky I hadn't mentioned it to her.

I leaned over and whispered to Jon. "Just imagine if she were mayor. Kids probably wouldn't be allowed to play in the park unless they had a letter from a parent saying their homework was done!"

Back in the classroom I stood in front of the bulletin board while everybody else lined up to go home. I found the article, picked somebody's stepped-on old math paper off the floor, and started taking notes.

By the time I finished, I was the only one left in the room. I grabbed my coat and took off down the hall.

Too late! Mrs. Murphy was already walking back to the room.

"Missed the bus again, Eric?" she said.

Again? I thought. It's just the second—O.K., third time this year.

"Do you want me to call your mom?" Mrs. Murphy asked.

I shook my head. "It's tax time. She's so busy doing people's taxes she can't even leave her desk to eat, half the time. I'll just walk over to her office. It's not that far."

Twenty blocks was far enough, actually, but Mrs. Murphy didn't need to know that. I could see her eyes narrowing as she tried to figure out what to do with me.

"Call first and O.K. it with your mom," she said.

I had to think fast while I punched in the number. Mom was not going to be thrilled with my missing the bus. But she might be too busy to pay much attention. When she was concentrating on something, she had this way of nodding and saying um-hmm to anything.

To anything.

When I get a really good idea, it makes the hairs on the back of my neck stand up. They were standing up now.

"Mom," I said. "Mom, I'm coming over to your office, O.K.? I've got something I want to talk to you about."

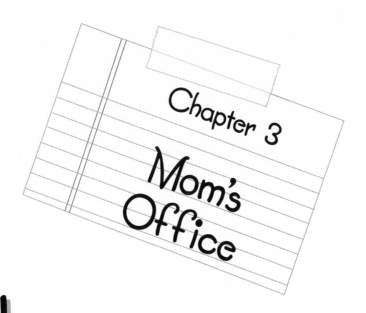

Chapter 3
Mom's Office

I stepped outside and looked off into the distance, toward my mom's office. Twenty blocks is not a death march, but it's no picnic, either. I hoisted my backpack onto both shoulders and started walking. At least I had plenty of time to think about what I was going to say. My backpack got heavier and heavier as the blocks changed from houses and swing sets to shops and businesses. Still I didn't stop, not even to look at the cookies in the window of French's Bakery. By the time I opened the door with the little tinkly bell at Clark Accounting, I was ready.

I had the waiting room to myself, so I sat down and pulled my math book out of my backpack. I knew my mom would be coming out of her office in a few minutes, and I wanted to look good.

Sure enough, not three minutes had gone by before she opened her door and looked out at me.

"Everything all right?" she asked.

"Everything's cool," I answered. "I just had an idea I wanted to talk to you about."

"Hmm," she said. She studied my face like a bug under a microscope. "I'll talk to you when I finish up with the Parkers."

I did all my math and had started my social studies definitions when the bell tinkled again. A tall, thin woman with a briefcase came in and sat in a chair across from me. This meant Mom wouldn't want to talk to me very long. That could be bad or good. I didn't know which.

Just then, an older couple came out of Mom's office. A white-haired woman held a huge pile of papers and envelopes. The man with her had a fat folder in his hands, too. The briefcase lady looked at Mom and smiled, probably hoping she'd be next.

"O.K., Eric," Mom said, and I followed her into her office.

I sat down on the edge of a chair in front of Mom's desk. She's got a few of these water toys on her desk that make cool designs with different colored water or sand when you tip them over. I turned them upside down, one by one.

"Well, Eric?" Mom asked. She reached for the mouse and clicked on something on her computer.

I could tell she was impatient. I had counted on her being busy. Busy was good. But impatient was

"You could make a big difference in this town, Mom."

dangerous. Maybe this was bad timing after all.

"I'm sorry, Mom," I said. "I know I shouldn't be bothering you here at work when you're this busy, but I was so upset I just had to come and talk to you about it."

That got her attention. She looked right up. "Did something happen at school?"

"School's fine, Mom. It's about the park. Lenox Field. The city council is selling it!"

I could see Mom relax. She began clicking away on her computer again as I talked. "And it's all Caitlin's uncle's fault. It was his idea."

"I'm not surprised," Mom said as she started leafing through a stack of papers. "I swear sometimes I think that man considers this town to be his own personal set of building blocks to do with as he sees fit."

Wow. This was going better than I had dreamed. She didn't like Caitlin's uncle either. "Sounds like we need a new mayor around here," I said.

Click, click, click went the mouse. "We certainly do," Mom said. She put her fingers on the keyboard and started typing.

"You'd make a great mayor, Mom," I said. "You're organized, responsible . . ." I tried to think of all the words my teacher used on my report card. Unfortunately, they were things I was supposed to improve, but right now they were just the words I needed.

Mom studied the computer screen.

"You could make a big difference in this town, Mom."

"Thanks, Eric," she said, never taking her eyes off the screen. "I'll try to do that. Could you tell Mrs. Ferguson she can come in now? And call your dad and see when he's bringing my dinner. You can get a ride home with him then."

I backed out of Mom's office, her words ringing in my ears. "I'll try to do that," she had said. She's going to do it! I thought. She's going to run for mayor! At least she said she would try. I looked at her one more time before I stepped out into the hallway. There was just one little question buzzing around in my head like a fly around a cow on a hot day. Did she really know what she had said? Maybe I should say something else.

No, I decided. No sense complicating things.

"Go ahead, Mrs. Ferguson," I said to the brief-case lady. "My mom is ready for you."

Mrs. Ferguson stood up and smiled. "Thank you, young man," she said. "Your mom's the best in town, you know."

I smiled back. If you think she's good at doing taxes, I thought, just wait till you see how good she is at being mayor!

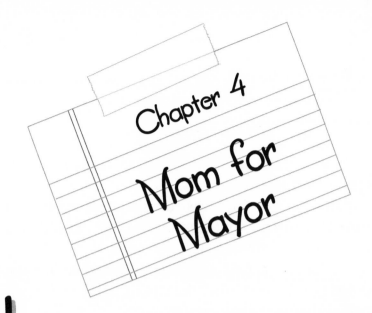

Chapter 4

Mom for Mayor

I had one more chance to talk to Mom about running for mayor when I helped Dad carry in her dinner. We stepped past a waiting couple and into the workroom. Mom was eating Chinese this time, and we had all these little white boxes with metal handles.

"Do we get Chinese, too?" I asked.

"Just the fortune cookies," Dad said, clearing a spot for the boxes next to the copy machine. "It's leftover lasagna for us."

That would be leftover, store-bought, frozen lasagna. Cooking is not my dad's favorite hobby.

Mom came out of her office, sniffed the food, and smiled.

"So, Mom," I said.

"Make sure he does his homework," she said over my head to Dad. "And make him look in his backpack to see if he has any. I swear that backpack is a black hole where homework disappears and is never seen again."

Very funny.

"I'm taking care of it, Liz," Dad said. "No more report card surprises."

Here we go. This was not going to be a good time to bring up anything. In fact, this would be a good time to will myself invisible.

"What about any projects?" she asked. "It's the projects we don't find out about until the night before that make me crazy."

She must be thinking about the dam we built for the science fair. Or maybe the model of Jamestown we built out of milk cartons. I turned away and opened a fortune cookie. FUTURE PROJECT BRINGS ADVENTURE. It was a sign! I knew it. I rolled the fortune up and stuffed it in my pocket. I'd show it to Mom some other time, when the words "future project" wouldn't automatically make her think of homework.

We rode home to icky lasagna in a car that still smelled like great food. Dad wanted to quiz me on my times tables, after having heard the Save Eric From Slacking speech. I wanted to talk about the park.

"Six times seven," he said.

"Forty-two. Dad, did you know the city's selling Lenox Field?"

"I guess I heard something about it. Seven times nine."

"Sixty-three. But it's the only park anywhere near our house. Don't you think somebody should do something about it?"

"What do you think somebody should do? Eleven times eleven."

"Dad, we're working on decimals right now, not multiplying," I complained. "And I think somebody who cares about the park should get on city council and change their minds."

I watched Dad's face as we drove along. If I want to know what I'll look like when I grow up, I just look at him. From our straight brown hair and brown eyes to our double-jointed fingers, we're a pretty close match.

Dad kept his eyes straight on the road. He didn't say anything for a minute. Then he said, "I know we used to go to the park when you were little. We had some fun, Eric. But there are more important things in life than swings and slides." He turned and looked at me. "Eleven times one point one. If you're working on decimals, you'll be working on multiplying them, too."

I sighed. Maybe Dad sees himself when he looks at me. Maybe that's why he's always trying to make me be perfect, like when you look at yourself in the mirror and pat down the hair that's sticking up or wipe the ketchup off your face. The only thing is, sometimes I'm afraid I may never be perfect enough for him.

"I don't know," I answered, grateful we were pulling into our driveway.

I called Jon as soon as I got home. "It's all set," I said. "My mom's going to run for mayor." I spoke quietly into the kitchen phone. Dad was in the living room watching the History Channel, and I just didn't want to hear his Ten Important Reasons for why Mom should not run for mayor and why I should be spending more time on my homework.

"She can't run for mayor," Jon answered back. "I looked it up on the city's Web site. In our town, people run for city council. Usually the person who gets the most votes gets to be mayor."

"Like I said," I told him. "My mom's going to be mayor."

"O.K., then," said Jon.

"There's just one problem," I said.

Jon groaned. "Oh, here it comes. You attract problems like garbage attracts flies. What is it?"

"Hey, it's not that big a problem," I said. "It's just that, well, my mom is really busy right now and she needs our help. So . . . what do we do?"

"Just a second," he said. "Let me get back to that Web site."

I wound and unwound myself in the phone cord while I waited. Finally, Jon came back on the line.

"O.K.," he said. "The first thing your mom has to do is go down to City Hall and get petitions."

"What are petitions?" I asked.

"It's something people have to sign, I guess," said Jon. "It says here you have to get seventy-five people to sign them."

I figured there must be seventy-five people who want to save Lenox Field. "We'll get those petitions tomorrow," I said. After I hung up, I sat by the phone, thinking. This was going to be the biggest project I had ever tackled—bigger than that model of Jamestown; bigger than my model dam.

I took a deep breath. I knew I wasn't very good at getting projects done. At least that's what my mom and dad and Mrs. Murphy would all say. But this project was too important to mess up. I went in my room and started searching through closets and drawers.

I finally found what I was looking for—a report folder that wasn't already covered with spaceship drawings. I opened the brass fasteners and put in a stack of notebook paper. On the top line of the first page, I printed, MOM FOR MAYOR. I skipped a line, put the next day's date, March 15, and wrote "Get petitions." I flipped through the blank sheets until I got to the last page. On the very last line of the last page, I wrote, MOM WINS THE ELECTION!

Now I just had to make it happen.

Chapter 5
City Hall

I could hardly wait for school to end the next day. Jon's mom picked us up and gave us a ride to the library, which just happened to be across the street from City Hall. We sat together in a corner behind the magazine racks, planning what to do.

"I can't believe you talked me into this," Jon whispered. He had a copy of the newspaper article about the city council election in front of him.

"It's no big deal," I said. "It's simple. We just go across the street to the city hall and pick up the petitions for my mom."

"But we're fifth graders," said Jon. "What makes you think they'll give them to us, anyway? And if it's no big deal, why were you so desperate for me to go with you?" He was running his fingers through his hair about every other sentence, a sure sign he was nervous.

"I need you to be my interpreter in case they start using all these words like 'petition' and 'nominating' and 'registered,'" I said, pointing to the article.

"I still think your mom should be doing this," Jon said.

I ignored him and started studying the article carefully.

"Eric . . ."

I avoided looking up.

"Eric, look at me," he said. "Is your mom completely aware that she's running for city council?"

I raised my head, turned, and looked straight at Jon. "She said it was a good idea," I said. "She said she'd try."

Jon studied my face, but I didn't turn away. "I don't know," he said. "It just doesn't seem—"

Before he could say another word, I stood up, grabbed him by the arm, and said, "Let's go. We'll get more done if we do it instead of just talk about it."

A few minutes later we were walking up the steps of City Hall. Lots of people before us had walked up these steps. You could tell by how they were kind of worn down in the middle. It was exciting. I felt like I was walking into history.

We started down a long, empty hallway, quieter even than the library. I read the gold lettering on each glass door we passed. Three doors down on the right I saw the words CITY CLERK.

"That's it. That's what we want," said Jonathan. I turned the knob. "Here we go."

We walked up to the counter and waited. An older woman stood off to one side, opening and closing file-cabinet drawers. Her glasses rested dangerously low on her nose. Maybe that's why she had them hooked to a chain around her neck. A younger woman had her back to us, talking on the phone.

"I'll be with you in a minute," said the file-cabinet lady. She closed the drawer with a *thwack*, turned, and studied us over the rims of her glasses. "Bike licenses are down the hall," she said, turning back to her files.

"But we're not here for bike licenses," I said. "We're here to pick up some of . . . um . . . to pick up those . . ."

"Petitions," whispered Jon.

". . . those petitions you need to run for city council."

The woman turned back to us and crossed her arms.

"For your mother," Jon whispered, poking me in the side.

"They're for my mother," I said. "For Elizabeth Clark."

The woman just stood there, staring at me. My cheeks were burning. I cleared my throat and stood up tall. "I'm her campaign manager."

I turned the knob. "Here we go."

I thought I almost saw her smile, but in the next second, she was all serious, like Mrs. Murphy before a big test. She folded her hands and placed them on the counter.

"I'm sure your mother is lucky to have such an eager supporter," she said, "but if she is truly interested in running for city council, she needs to come down here herself to pick up her petitions."

"But Mrs. Clark asked us to come."

I turned and looked at Jon. I couldn't believe it. Jon panics about speaking to an audience, but he wasn't finished yet.

"Mrs. Clark does people's taxes, and right now is her busiest time of the year," Jon went on. "She works from morning till night."

"That's right," I said, snapping out of my speechlessness. "Lots of times she eats lunch and dinner right at her desk."

"Well, hello, Jonny." The young woman hung up the phone and stepped over to the counter. "I used to baby-sit this fine young man," she said to the file lady. "He's a really smart kid."

Jon blushed, but he spoke up. "We're here to pick up petitions for Eric's mom, Liz Clark, so she can run for city council."

"I heard a little of your conversation," she said. "You know Jonathan, we have that rule so that people don't just come in here and take out petitions for friends they think ought to run."

"Or Smokey the Bear, for that matter," grumbled the file lady. "We want candidates who are sure this is what they want to do."

"But she wants to do this," Jon insisted. "She said so."

"And if she has to wait until tax season is over, she won't be able to get a good head start," I added. I avoided looking at Jonathan. I didn't want my surprise at what he said to make the ladies suspicious.

"Please, Maggie," Jon begged, his face now a disturbing shade of red.

Maggie sighed. "Well, Mrs. Foster, it looks like we've got a problem here." She thought for a moment. "It's our custom that candidates come here in person, but it's not a law. What do you think?"

Mrs. Foster looked at Maggie. She looked at us. "Can you vouch for Mrs. Clark's intent to run for city council? She's serious? This is not some here-today-gone-tomorrow whim?"

Maggie looked at Jon. "Is she serious?" she asked. "She really wants to run?"

"Absolutely!" Jon exclaimed. "Right, Eric?"

"Sure, right!" I said, trying to match his enthusiasm. She'll want to run for city council, I thought, just as soon as she knows about it.

Chapter 6
My Dad

On the way back to the library, Jon practically crowed. "We did it! We did it!"

I slapped him on the back. "You were really something in there," I said. "I think you could have pulled that off without my help at all. And by the way, Jonny," I said, poking him in his ribs, "how come you never told me about your cute baby-sitter? The only baby-sitter I ever remember was your aunt who liked opera music."

Jon ignored me and spread the petitions and instructions out on the library table.

"Hey, why don't we ask people to sign them right now?" I said, looking around and starting to count the number of people in the library.

"Eric, don't you ever pay attention?" Jon asked. "They told us you have to be a registered voter to pass around these city council petitions. It says so right here." He pointed to the last paragraph on a page of directions.

"O.K., O.K.," I said. "You know, sometimes you sound so much like Mrs. Murphy it's scary." I looked up at the clock. "Anyway, my dad should be here in a couple minutes." I scooped up the papers and put them in my backpack.

"By the way," I said, walking to the door, "let's not say anything to my dad about this city council thing just yet. I don't know exactly how much Mom has told him."

Jon stopped dead in his tracks. He stared at me. "I knew it. I knew it. This is all your idea. Your mom doesn't know anything about this yet, does she." It was a statement, not a question.

I searched for the right words.

"You tricked me!" Jon exploded. "And I made a fool of myself back there. 'Oh yes, Maggie, oh yes. Mrs. Clark wants to do this. She said so. Absolutely!'" He paced back and forth in the lobby.

"But she did say it was a good idea," I said. "She did, honest. And when I told her she could really make a difference in this town, she said she'd try."

Jon looked at me. His eyes narrowed. "But . . . ?" he asked.

I turned away and looked out the door and down the street. "But I don't think she was really listening." I sighed. "I don't know if she knew what she was saying."

"Your mom doesn't know anything about this . . ."

Jon groaned. "Terrific. It's Bert and Ernie time all over again."

My dad's car pulled up.

"Don't worry, Jon," I said. "If she thought it was a good idea without thinking about it, she'll really think it's a good idea when she really thinks about it." I pushed the library door open and stepped outside.

Jon followed, shaking his head and snorting. "You make about as much sense as my aunt's talking parrot. Still, I know your mom would be great on city council. She was a great den mother in Cub Scouts."

We climbed into the backseat of Dad's old Grand Prix. A light rain had started to fall, one of those early spring rains that makes you feel cold, all the way to the middle of your bones. The windshield wipers kept trying to slap the raindrops away as we drove through town. I watched as the streetlights came on.

Dad started raining parent questions on me like, "How was your day?" and "Do you have any homework?" I was the windshield wiper, slapping them away. "Fine." "Not much." The less Dad knew right now, the better.

"Look, there's Lenox Field," said Jon.

I slapped my hand to my forehead. I couldn't help it. This was just way too close to the topic of the city council election. I tried to give Jon a warning glare, but the passing streetlights didn't give off enough light to be much help. Jon kept on going.

"I remember the times you took me there to play with Eric," he said, leaning forward toward the front seat. "It was great, Mr. Clark. You pretended that we were flying to Africa on the swings. Then we looked for elephants in the woods and slid down an elephant's trunk on the slide. Eric must get his imagination from you."

If only there was a way Jon could accidentally fall out of the car at this very moment. His next sentence would probably tell Dad why we needed the park, and then the very next sentence would be why it was so great that my mom was running for city council.

Dad turned the wipers up faster. It was a real downpour now.

"A little imagination is one thing," Dad said. "But you can't live in a fantasy world. When I'm changing someone's brakes at work, I'd better not be pretending I'm repairing the Starship *Enterprise*."

My mom and dad and my teachers have all been on a Down With Daydreaming campaign since I was in second grade. It was like a sub-category in the Improve Eric's Report Card plan.

Dad stopped at a stop sign and turned to look straight at me. "And when Eric's doing a math paper, he would be much better off if he didn't cover it with aliens."

We drove a block farther and pulled into Jon's driveway.

"Well, thanks for the ride, Mr. Clark," he said, opening the door before the car had even stopped. He raised his eyebrows and gave me this I'm-really-sorry-but-I-just-dropped-a-live-grenade-in-your-car-by-accident-and-I-guess-I-must-be-leaving look. Then he ran for his front door as fast as he could, and I don't think it was because it was raining.

The thing is, Dad really does have this wild imagination. I mean, this is a guy who builds metal animal statues out of old machine and car parts and sells them at art fairs—cats with nails for whiskers and metal gear parts for bodies, dogs with tails made from big old springs. So just what did Dad draw on his math papers when he was in school?

"Dinner's ready," he said as we bumped over the curb and into our driveway. "I already took some to your mom. She won't be home till late."

"Pizza maybe?" I asked, coming out from under my own personal thundercloud long enough to feel hope.

"No, I put some leftovers together. It'll be great."

Hope fizzled. This is where my dad's imagination got him into trouble, in my opinion. "What is it?" I asked, not really wanting to know.

"It's a kind of lasagna-green-pea soup," he said.

He can get away with stuff like this, but I'm supposed to keep my imagination in a box? I started to worry that if Mom did win the election, Dad would be in charge of more dinners.

We ran in the back door and hung our dripping coats up on hooks. I planted myself in front of the stove to warm up. I peeked in the steaming pot. It was lasagna, all right. Only it was green. And runny.

I sighed. Sometimes great heroes in American history made sacrifices for the good of their country. I put the lid back on. If being a hero and saving my park meant eating green lasagna-pea soup, then I would just have to do it.

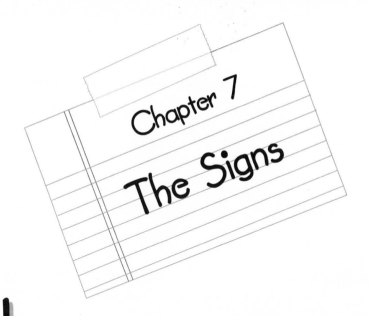

Chapter 7
The Signs

It's amazing how fast time can go by when you know you need to do something and you start putting it off. How long had it been since Jon and I picked up the petitions? Two weeks? Three?

I sat at the kitchen table with my MOM FOR MAYOR notebook open in front of me. I had a few things checked off my list of things to do, which was good. But there was no check at all in front of the most important one.

I pushed the notebook away and looked through a catalog I had picked up at the sign shop. I rode over there on my bike the day after we got our petitions. This catalog was pretty cool. I couldn't believe all the things you could buy when you were running for office—pens, pencils, key chains, all with your name on them.

The glow-in-the-dark Frisbees were great. I really

wanted them. I could just imagine giving one to every kid in my class. I could see them sailing right over Caitlin's head at recess. Then I saw the price. No way. I had already used up all my money last week when I ordered some yard signs for Mom.

Mom. The very thought sent a shiver down my back. I stood up and looked out the window. I really have to tell her, I thought. I had been waiting for the perfect moment—one when I wasn't in too much trouble.

Maybe some people have days when they're not in trouble for their grades, or their messy bedroom, or the glass of milk left on top of the TV. I was looking forward to having one of those days. Someday.

I looked around the kitchen. Oops. I picked my coat and backpack up off the floor. I've got to tell her today, no matter what, I decided.

I started pacing circles around the kitchen table. I worked on my speech.

"Mom, I have something very important to talk to you about." Hmm. I turned around, changed direction, and tried again.

"Mom, our city needs good people running it." That sounded good. I kept going. "People who believe kids need parks, people who—"

I heard the door open and then slam shut. I turned around and found myself face to face with my mother.

"Eric Nathaniel Clark!"

"Eric Nathaniel Clark!"

Uh-oh. This was three-name trouble. What had I done this time? Mom had something in her hands. When I realized what it was, I felt the blood drain out of my face and then rush back to my cheeks like some wild blood roller coaster. She was holding a sign, a bright orange sign with black letters. It said, LIZ CLARK FOR CITY COUNCIL.

"Where . . . where did you get that?" I blurted out. I searched every corner of my brain for a simple explanation.

"Where?" Mom exploded. "I thought you of all people would know the answer to that question, seeing as how it's your name at the bottom of the order!" She waved a pink form in front of my eyes. "I thought it was some kind of mistake until I saw that." Her eyes pinned me down like a butterfly in a bug collection. "One of my clients works at the printing company. He dropped about fifty of these off at my office today. He wished me luck. Said he'd vote for me!"

I gulped. There was no way out.

"So, young man, it seems to me that a better question is why? Why on earth would you pull such a harebrained scheme? What were you thinking? And where did you get the money?"

"I used the money I was saving for Rollerblades." I answered the easy question first. "And I did it because I knew you would be great on city council. I thought you could save the park."

"The park? This is about the park?" Mom took off her coat and shoved up her sleeves, a sure sign she was really steamed.

"But, Mom, we talked about it at your office, remember?" I willed her to remember. "And you said the mayor thinks this town is his own personal set of building blocks, and I said you could really make a difference, and you said you'd try. Remember?"

Mom crossed her arms. "I remember that I most certainly did not say, 'You know, son, I believe I'll run for city council. Would you please order some signs for me?' Why didn't you tell me?"

Good question. I sighed. "I was going to, Mom, really, I just—"

A knock on the door saved me right in the middle of my squirming. I raced to answer it.

"Look, Eric!" Jon stood at the door, waving papers in his hand. "My mom took petitions around our neighborhood and already got thirty names!"

Oh no! I'd forgotten Jon had taken a couple of petitions home with him. I heard my mom step up behind me.

"Oh hi, Mrs. Clark." I saw Jon look up at her face. He looked at me. "You didn't tell her? You said you were going to tell her." He looked back and forth between the two of us again. "You . . . did tell her. But she's not . . . pleased. Um, I think I'll be going now." Jon shoved the petitions into my hands, jumped on his bike, and was gone.

Mom shook her head. "Petitions?" she said, taking the papers from me. She looked them over. "These look official. But how did you ever . . ." She sighed. "What a mess. And I have to get back to the office. I just came home to find out face to face what you were up to this time." She shook her head again. Then she looked me straight in the eye. "But let's be clear on one thing," she said. "I am not, N-O-T, not running for city council!" She went out the door and slammed it behind her.

I felt like a popped balloon. I leaned against the refrigerator and slid slowly to the ground. Oh, am I ever in the doghouse, I thought. Probably for life!

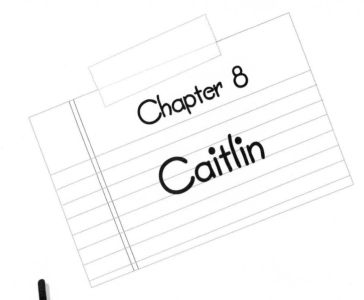

Chapter 8

Caitlin

Jon beat me to the bus stop the next day. I tried to read his face to see if he was upset about the whole not-telling-my-mom thing.

"Page three," he said, and he slapped a newspaper into my hands.

I scanned the page and groaned. Halfway down, an article announced, "Twelve Candidates Take Out Petitions." There was my mom's name and address.

"Do I smell cooked goose?" Jon asked.

"That's what we had for dinner last night when my dad got home, believe me," I said. I sighed. I could just imagine how much fun dinner would be tonight after my parents saw this.

"So tell me," Jon said, crossing his arms. "Am I supposed to go back to all those people who signed petitions and tell them it was a mistake?"

"No, don't do that," I said. "Mom just needs time to think this over. It'll be all right. You'll see."

"Really?" Jon asked. "Right about now I'd be looking for some friend or relative in, say, Alaska that I could stay with if I were you."

Secretly I agreed, but I'd never admit it. I clapped Jon on the back. "You worry too much," I said. "Everything's going to be fine."

Everything was fine for about twenty minutes, until the bus dumped us off at school. As soon as I walked into the classroom, Mrs. Murphy came over to talk to me.

"Eric, I see your mother is running for city council," she said. "What a wonderful opportunity for you to witness democracy in action."

I knew it. Mrs. Murphy loved this stuff. It wasn't too often that Mrs. Murphy found "wonderful" things to discuss with me. I decided I was going to make the most of this.

"That's right, Mrs. Murphy," I said, completely ignoring the warning look on Jon's face. "I already learned about people signing petitions."

"I learned about that years ago." Caitlin just had to butt in.

Mrs. Murphy turned around and looked at Caitlin. "Perhaps you could give Eric a few pointers on campaigning," she said. "His mother's running for city council." She turned to talk to another student before she could hear what Caitlin said.

"Your mother doesn't have a chance," Caitlin told me. "She doesn't know anything about politics or running a city. My uncle Roger said so himself."

Caitlin's nose tipped up into the air. It reminded me of how my grandpa would say, "Go out in the rain like that and you could drown." I might have laughed at the thought if I hadn't been so mad.

"At least she knows better than to sell the only park in our neighborhood," I said. "And my mother says your uncle uses this town like his own set of building blocks. And he has to be stopped!" I threw that in for good measure.

Caitlin's glare made me wonder if she had perfected that lightning-bolt-from-the-eye thing I saw once in a video game.

"Eric Clark," she said, spitting out her words, "if your mother knew anything, she'd know the city is working on turning one of their empty lots into a new park to replace the one by your house."

I was speechless. I'm never speechless.

"Where?" asked Jon.

"Over by Eighteenth and Ash."

Jon and I groaned at the same time. That was across a highway, on the other side of the industrial park, at least two miles away.

"Fat lot of good that will do us," I said.

"It might as well be on the moon," Jon added.

"Too bad for you," said Caitlin. "That's just how it's going to be."

"Not if my mom can help it," I said. I crossed my arms and tried my best to give her back that same lightning-bolt stare. "Not only is she going to get on city council, she's going to beat your stupid old uncle and be the new mayor! Now, if you'll excuse me, I have work to do." I pulled out my chair and sat down with *a thump.*

"Ow! My foot! My foot!" Caitlin screamed.

I looked down. Somehow the leg of my chair was on her foot. I jumped up.

"You did that on purpose!" she cried.

Before I knew what had happened, Mrs. Murphy was at my desk, and I had lost recess. Again. I gritted my teeth. Caitlin smiled as she sat down.

At recess time, I could see her out the window, her fat ponytail bouncing up and down as she jumped rope.

Oh, her poor injured foot, I thought.

I looked down at the piece of paper on my desk. I was supposed to write one page explaining what happened and what I should have done. Suddenly, I had an idea.

"Mrs. Murphy?" I asked. "How about if I write a letter to the editor about why the city shouldn't sell Lenox Field? That's what Caitlin and I were arguing about."

Mrs. Murphy thought for a moment. "Lenox Field. I remember playing there when I was a child." She looked out the window. "That's a good idea,"

"OW! My foot! My foot!"

she said. "In fact," she went on, still looking out the window, toward the girls with their jump ropes, "I think I'll have Caitlin write one, too, explaining her side. Go on out when you finish it, and tell Caitlin I want to see her."

Mrs. Murphy went back to her work, and I reached into my desk. I pulled out the letter to the editor I had started three weeks ago when I first heard the news about Lenox Field. It was on my MOM FOR MAYOR check-off list, but I hadn't gotten around to finishing it yet.

I looked at what I had written so far.

Dear Editor:

Lenox Field is my favorite place in the whole world. It's where kids play and fly kites and kick a soccer ball around.

Not bad. I picked up my pencil and started writing. I got more enthusiastic with every word I wrote.

Selling the park is a terrible idea. Kids need parks! Don't kick us out into the streets. Putting in a substitute park over on Ash won't help out any of the kids in my neighborhood until they're old enough to drive. Don't let the mayor and the city council take away our park!

Yours for justice,
Eric Nathaniel Clark

I looked at my letter. Mom is going to make such a terrific mayor, I thought. Then, like a cloud covering the sun, the actual truth came back to me. My mother was not, N-O-T, not running for city council. I stopped and chewed on my pencil.

At least, not yet.

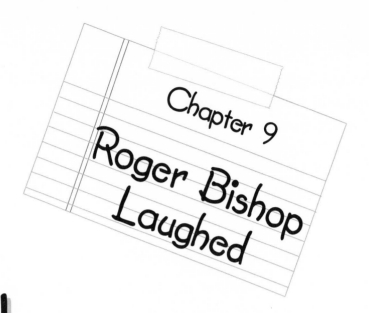

Chapter 9
Roger Bishop Laughed

I sat at the desk in my bedroom after school and pulled out my MOM FOR MAYOR folder. I ran my finger down my things-to-do list: Get petitions—check. Order signs—check. Write a letter to the editor—I put a little check. I finished it at school, but I still had to mail it. Tell Mom—that sure didn't work out as well as I had hoped, but, check. Get Mom's name in the newspaper. I put a check in the little box in front of that one, too, and sighed. It looked like everything was under control.

I just had to talk Mom into running for city council. I turned the page and started a new list. I titled it WAYS TO CONVINCE MOM TO RUN.

1. Promise I'll get straight A's on my report card.

I thought about my last science test. Maybe that wasn't such a good plan.

2. Offer to do dishes every night.

I thought hard about that one. This was going to be painful.

3. Write Mom a letter.

That might actually work. And Jon could help me think of reasons, and maybe he'd sign it, too.

This was such a good idea that I started for the phone to call Jon. It rang just before I picked it up. I bet it was Jon. Great minds think alike.

"Hey," I said.

"Eric."

The voice on the other end was my mother. I almost dropped the phone. I knew I'd hear about the newspaper story tonight, but she wasn't supposed to be home till after nine o'clock. People had one week left to finish doing their taxes, and Mom was really, really busy. I never thought she'd call.

"Eric?" she said again.

"Hi, Mom," I answered.

"Eric, fourteen different people have called me at work today, offering to help with my campaign."

I gulped.

"Two people actually came into my office to offer their support in person."

"Uh, wow, you're pretty popular, Mom." I backed up until I found myself pressed against the wall like an animal caught in a trap.

"There was an article about the council race in this morning's paper."

Here it comes. I shut my eyes.

"And then, this afternoon, Roberta Carter stopped in."

I squeezed my eyes together, trying to remember who Roberta Carter was and why it might be important.

"She works at the Main Street Diner."

I still didn't have a clue.

"She waited on a table of businessmen, one of whom was none other than Roger Bishop himself."

I started to sweat. I could hear the anger in my mom's voice.

"They were talking about the city council elections, and someone brought up my name."

I held my breath.

"Roger Bishop laughed. He said I was another one of those bored housewives trying to impress her friends. He said I had no political experience and that being a scout leader hardly qualifies a person to run a city."

"He said all that?"

"Every word, according to Roberta." The more my mom spoke, the louder her voice became. "He said it was probably just a passing fancy. He doubted I'd even hand in my petitions."

I looked at our phone to see if smoke was coming out of it. Oh, my mom was hot. The level of mad I got last night was nothing compared to this. I only wondered how much of this new mad would be pointed at Mr. Bishop and how much would bounce off onto me for getting her into this mess in the first place.

"Mom?" I said.

"Passing fancy!" she exploded. "Who does this big blow-hard think he is? It just so happens I went to plenty of council meetings before I started working full time. He might as well have suggested I join a quilting bee or a health spa." She paused.

"Eric?" she said.

I had no idea what might be coming. "Yes?" I managed to squeak.

"I'm running for city council."

When Mom works late, Dad and I have dinner together. Then, when Mom gets home, they sit at the table and have a snack while they talk. Sometimes, if it's not too late, I get in on the snack, too.

Tonight was another late night for Mom, but I came down in my pajamas to hear what she and Dad would have to say.

"Liz, I'm only worried that you're taking on too much," Dad said. "You can't let certain people pressure you into this."

I didn't know if Dad meant me or Roger Bishop, but I tried to be as invisible as I could at that moment.

"Jim, I've thought this through. I'm not a scout leader anymore, and my term as PTA treasurer ends before the election. And as much as some people

"I'm running for city council."

may have tried to pressure me into this," Mom said, looking straight at me, "this is something I've been thinking about for a long time. Our council has made some decisions that have made my blood boil."

"Let's see . . ." Dad started counting on his fingers. "There was the time your scout troop was charged an entry fee in the Swingin' Summer Festival parade. . . . Oh, and the time they canceled the town's annual fireworks to save money and then redecorated the offices in City Hall. I've seen the steam, I admit it." Dad sighed. "So what's next?"

This was my cue. "I've got it all written down," I said. I handed Mom my MOM FOR MAYOR folder. She and Dad looked at it together. Dad ran his finger down the checklist.

"You did this yourself?" he asked.

"You sent a letter to the editor?" said Mom. She looked at me like she had just opened our refrigerator and discovered a fancy dinner on fine china complete with candlelight. "You did this yourself?" she asked. "It's so well organized."

I wish they hadn't been so surprised that I could pull this off, but I guess I deserved it.

Mom tapped her finger on number three. "Although I really think "Tell Mom" should have been number one." She looked at Dad. "I think we have our campaign manager," she said. Then she turned back to me. "What's next?"

I turned the page and showed her. "Get seventy-five people to sign the petitions," I read. "I, uh, guess you already know that's partly done, thanks to Jon's mom, but we need more."

I pointed to the next step. "Hand in petitions. They said you have to do that yourself in person no matter what. And they have to be in by May third."

"That gives us a couple weeks," said Dad. "And then after that?"

The rest of the page was blank. "That's as far as I got," I said.

Dad pulled a pen out of his pocket and began to write. "We'll need fliers," he said.

This sounded too cool. "You mean those airplanes that pull a message behind them?" I asked.

Mom laughed out loud, and Dad must have been laughing on the inside, because his shoulders were shaking.

"Pamphlets," he explained. "Brochures."

Right. I knew that.

"My sister Debby can take the pictures," Mom said.

"We'll need newspaper ads, too," Dad said. He picked up his ice-cream spoon and tapped it absent-mindedly on the table. "Are you sure you want to go through with all of this? It's going to cost quite a bit."

My mom's brain is a regular calculator. She was ready with the answer. "I thought that through. If we spend a weekend at the lake this summer instead of a week, that will help some."

"And we could give up eating out," said Dad.

All of a sudden this conversation was getting out of hand. All I could see were cheeseburgers with wings, flying away. What had I started?

Chapter 10
Bulldozers

The next day I took my time walking through Lenox Field on the way to my bus stop. I paid attention to each tree, the overgrown path through the woods, the way the sun reflected off the metal slide. I looked at each piece and part of Lenox Field like it was mine, like I owned it. I felt like I owned it. Mom was going to be mayor, and everything would be fine.

And then I saw the bulldozers. My stomach dropped down to my toes. I forgot all about the bus and school and went running over. Two guys sat in a big pickup truck next to the bulldozers, drinking coffee.

"Hey, you can't do this!" I shouted.

The guy on the driver's side rolled down his window. "What's the matter, kid?" he asked.

"You can't tear down this park," I cried. "It's not

60

fair! You've got to wait. My mom's running for city council. She'll never let anybody tear this down."

The driver opened his door and stepped out. He was one big guy. I had a feeling he wouldn't even need a bulldozer. He could probably rip those trees out with his bare hands.

"There won't be many trees left to save come election time in November," he said. "We'll have all the streets and sewers in by then." He poured his coffee on the ground with a *splat*. "Come on, Joe. Let's get started."

I would have thrown myself in front of a tree if I thought it would do any good, but which tree? I couldn't save them all. I stood there, frozen, until I heard the motor start up. Then I took off running for home as fast as I could.

"Mom! Mom!" I cried as I tore into our house. "They've got bulldozers at the park. They're going to tear it down. You've got to stop them!"

Mom stood by the kitchen sink, dressed for the office. She held a piece of toast in one hand and the newspaper in the other. I stood there, panting. I knew she was ready to fly out the door. Would she have time to squeeze in stopping a couple of bulldozers?

Mom juggled her toast to her newspaper hand, picked up her mug, and took a gulp of tea. "I spent some time on the phone last night," she said. "Lenox Field was a done deal weeks ago. Bought

"There won't be many trees left to save . . . ."

and sold. It's out of our hands. The city doesn't own it anymore."

"But, Mom!" I fell back against a wall. I felt like *I'd* been bulldozed. "Why did you decide to run for mayor if you couldn't do anything about it?"

Mom rinsed out her cup and dried her hands. "There's more to being on city council than one park. Taxes, streets, businesses . . ." She picked her purse up off a chair and headed me toward the door, her hand on my back.

I thought about the money I had sunk into those yard signs and sighed. I hadn't given up all that cash for streets and businesses.

Mom's hand patted my back as we walked out to the car. "Don't look so glum," she said. "There's the matter of the new park."

I shook my head. "But the new park's miles from here, Caitlin said, across the highway, on Ash Street." I slouched down into the car.

Mom turned the key, and we started backing down the driveway. "Nothing's been carved in stone," she said. "We can stop that and push for a better location."

"Like where?" I asked. I was still feeling grouchy. I didn't think any substitute park could be half as good. I could see the tops of the trees of Lenox Field in the distance, stretching above a row of houses as we drove past. Mom had chosen a different street than usual, farther away from the park.

I think she didn't want to make me feel worse by driving past the bulldozers. It didn't matter. I could hear their roar, a couple blocks away.

"The next city council meeting's in two weeks," Mom said. She turned down a street and headed away from school.

Had she forgotten where we were going? This was a pretty nice street, with big new houses.

She stopped in front of an empty lot. "What do you think?" she asked.

I looked at Mom, and then I looked back at the field. It wasn't very big. You could see clear through to the street on the other side. I could count the trees on one hand.

"It's farther away than Lenox Field, I know, but you could ride your bike here," she said. "There aren't any busy streets to cross."

She sounded like she was trying to sell it to me. I wasn't buying. "There's no room for baseball," I pointed out. "Or flying a kite. Or anything."

"Or anything?" Mom asked. "I thought someone with your imagination would be able to think of lots of possibilities for this land if the city decides to turn it into a park."

O.K. She had me there. Nobody questions my imagination. All of a sudden I could see cool new climbing equipment springing up here and there.

"But how do you know the city will be able to buy this lot?" I asked. I was afraid to get my hopes up.

"The city owns this land already. They've been talking about what to do with it for some time. So far Roger Bishop and his cronies have turned down every suggestion."

I studied my mom's face. Roger Bishop better look out. She had on her don't-argue-with-me-you-can't-possibly-win face.

"You're going to that council meeting, aren't you, Mom," I said. It wasn't even a question.

"I am," she replied. "And so are you."

Chapter 11
Kids Live Here, Too!

Two weeks should have been plenty of time to write my speech for the city council meeting, but fifteen minutes before we were supposed to go, I was still scratching things out and trying it a different way.

It's not that I didn't have ideas. I had lots of ideas. Like making a tree costume and standing up at the microphone and saying, "You killed my park," and falling over. I was sure that would get their attention. Mom said absolutely not.

Then I wrote this great song. I wrote "Lenox Field Is Falling Down" to the tune of "London Bridge Is Falling Down." They use catchy songs in ads to make you remember their product. Mom said no singing.

So all she left me with was words, and I wanted the very best words I could think of.

Mom called from the hallway. "Time to go."

I stuffed my index cards into my pocket. Before I knew it, Mom and I were walking into City Hall. I'd never been to a city council meeting before, but Mom's been to lots of them. I followed her down some steps into a large meeting room.

A handful of people sat in the folding chairs set up for the audience. A group of high-school students sat off to one side. I was a little disappointed. I was hoping for a bigger audience for my grand entrance into politics, as my mom had called it.

I looked at the people sitting behind the table at the front of the room. I had to read their little brass nameplates to see which one was Roger Bishop. As much as Caitlin talked about her uncle, I'd never seen him in person, never paid attention to his picture in the paper. I had expected a snaky-looking, beady-eyed man, maybe with a mustache that he twirled. Instead, he was a round, smiling man with wavy, white hair. The man next to him said something, and he threw back his head and laughed. It was a deep, hearty laugh. I would have liked him better snaky.

Mom said we'd have a chance to speak pretty early in the meeting, but it seemed like forever before they got through all their minutes and reports and whatever. Finally Roger Bishop said, "We'll now take comments from the audience. Please come up to the microphone and state your name."

An older lady got to the microphone ahead of me. She had something to say about the parking downtown. While she talked, my mouth dried up, and my hands got sweaty. Then she stepped away, and I was alone in front of the microphone. My heart was pounding, but I spoke right up. "My name is Eric Clark."

"Hold it," Roger Bishop said.

My mouth fell open. How could he stop me before I even had a chance to say anything? But then I noticed someone lowering the microphone so I could speak into it.

I started again. "My name is Eric Clark." I looked those council people in the eye. "I'm here to tell you about Lenox Field. Lenox Field was a lot more than a swing set and a slide and some woods. It was a place where a kid could have an adventure." I left my index cards in my pocket. I knew exactly what I wanted to say.

"Maybe you think a kid like me doesn't have any place up here talking to you, since I can't even vote. Yet. But somebody has to remind you that kids live here, too. And kids know a lot about parks, probably more than you do. When was the last time any of you went flying down a slide or sailing through the air on a swing?" I looked at Roger Bishop and knew for a fact he hadn't climbed up a slide any time recently. "When's the last time you even took a walk in the woods?

How could he stop me before I even had a chance
to say anything?

"For two weeks now I've watched the bulldozers knock down trees and rip up the swing and slide. You stole away an important piece of my life. Now it's up to you to find a better place for a new park, better than some piece of land too far away from my house to be of any use. It takes more than a sign to make a park a park. Thank you."

I walked back to my seat surrounded by the sound of whoops and cheers and clapping. Even the high-school kids were rooting for me. The council members looked at each other with raised eyebrows. They hadn't been expecting me, that's for sure. But it wasn't over yet. My mom was next.

"Members of the council," she began, "my name is Elizabeth Clark. I would like to suggest a solution to this park problem you have created."

Mom was great. She had facts. She had figures. She knew just how much the lights were going to cost for the baseball field, and how much money the city had made on the sale of Lenox Field. She even knew how much money the city would probably take in on taxes from the new houses. She explained why children in the Lenox Field neighborhood wouldn't be able to use a park on Ash Street. And then she told them exactly where the new park should be, how big it was, and what it would cost to develop. Go, Mom!

I guess other people in the audience agreed, because she got lots of clapping and cheering, too.

The council members whispered to each other. Finally Roger Bishop cleared his throat.

"Well. That was some presentation, ma'am. We've seen you here before, haven't we? Have you ever thought about running for city council?" he asked with a smile.

I knew what he was trying to do. He was trying to use his charm to get the topic away from the park.

My mom smiled back. "I am running for city council," she said. "I thought you already knew."

His smile faded. "I'm sorry. What did you say your name was?"

"Elizabeth Clark," Mom said. "I have thought the matter over carefully. Believe me when I say my decision is based on more than a passing fancy."

Roger Bishop sat back in his chair like he'd just had the wind knocked out of him.

"By the way," Mom continued, "my campaign theme will be, 'Our kids live here, too.'"

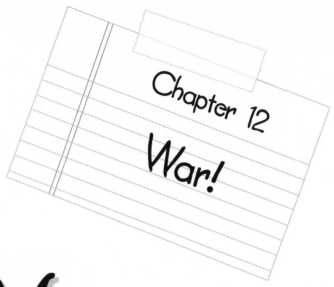

Chapter 12
War!

Mom might have surprised me when she took part of my speech and used it for her theme. But what didn't surprise me was seeing how she carried it out. My mother is one organized person. Even her spice rack is in alphabetical order. Mom went house to house around Lenox Field, talking to neighbors. She wrote letters and went to more council meetings.

Before I knew it, it was the middle of May, and the campaign was in full swing. Mom and Dad had election brochures printed up, and I took one to school. I showed it to Jon at the bus stop.

"I always knew your Mom would run for city council," said Jon. "She'll be great."

"The thing is," I said, "my parents have taken over. Look at this pamphlet." I waved it in his face.

"Just look at this picture," I went on. "They made me wear a tie! Our family picture makes us look like a family that never set foot in a park instead of a family that wants to save the park. I said we should get our picture taken standing in front of the piles of sewer pipes and backhoes at Lenox Field, but nobody listens to me."

"Eric," Jon said, "this whole thing was your idea. Obviously they listened to you."

"You'd never know it," I grumbled.

As soon as I got to school, I put the pamphlet up on the IN THE NEWS bulletin board. I put it right next to—well, slightly on top of Caitlin's letter to the editor. You could hardly call it a real letter to the editor, though. It looked to me like she had sent in the same report she had given in class about her wonderful uncle and his stupid baseball-field lights. I wrinkled my nose at it. Caitlin saw me and came over.

"Does your mother have all her petitions handed in?" she asked.

I knew she was expecting me to say no, hoping I'd say no. I looked at her with an icy gaze. At least I was hoping for something in the icy-gaze ball-park.

"Of course," I said. "I'll have you know people were calling us up to get petitions to sign."

Caitlin took a step back. Ha! That had surprised

her. No need for her to know it was just one of Mom's cousins who had called.

On my way to my desk, I started noticing the pencils. Three people were lined up at the pencil sharpener with them. Others had them on top of their desks—lime green with the words "Vote for Roger Bishop" in bright orange. Even Zac and Tyler had Roger Bishop pencils.

Zac gave me a guilty smile. "I lost all my other pencils," he said with a shrug, stuffing it into a mass of papers and books in his desk. Tyler was busy scraping Roger Bishop's name off with the edge of a ruler. That made me feel a little better. Still, I knew that if my mom was ever going to win the election, she was going to have to do a better job of selling herself. She was going to need my help.

The bell rang. I pulled out my reading book and listened while Mrs. Murphy talked about *Charlotte's Web*. I dug around in my desk and found two pencils. I tried writing "Vote for Liz" on them with a marker, but it just wiped off. Then I started making badges to pass out. I drew baseball bats on my notebook paper and wrote "Vote for Liz" on each one. When I had drawn twenty, I started cutting them out.

"Eric."

The voice of doom. I looked up. Mrs. Murphy was standing in front of me, arms crossed. I could see thoughts of a summer-long detention passing through her eyes.

I had to say something fast. "Mrs. Murphy, I'm trying to think of all the things I can do to help my mom get elected to city council so she can get us a new park. I know I was supposed to be reading along, but don't you think participating in . . . in . . . ." I looked at the chart on the wall. ". . . in the principles of democracy is more important than *Charlotte's Web*?"

I crossed my fingers and hoped with all my heart that *Charlotte's Web* wasn't her most favorite book in the whole world.

"Eric," she said, and there was no trace of a smile on her face. "If you had actually bothered to spend a little time reading *Charlotte's Web* you would see that Charlotte does a magnificent job of campaigning, in a way, for Wilbur the pig. However . . . ."

I held my breath, crossed my fingers, and tried to cross my toes.

". . . I think participating in an election like this is an important thing . . . ."

There was hope!

". . . and I would be happy to talk about it with you . . . ."

Yes!

". . . at recess time."

Aargh! Nothing had ever made me lose more recesses than this election.

By June, our IN THE NEWS bulletin board was crammed with articles. Twelve people were running for city council, but almost everything up there was about either my mom or Roger Bishop. That board had become a battle ground, and Caitlin and I were the armies on opposite sides. Caitlin made a point of posting every single newspaper article that mentioned her uncle. Every time she did, I'd shoot back with a newspaper article of my own.

Boom! She put up a newspaper ad for her uncle.

Bang! I put up an ad for my mom.

It was a tough war. There were way more articles about her uncle the mayor than about my mom. Our letters to the editor were up there, of course. Then lots of other people started writing in about building a new park to replace Lenox Field, and I put their letters up, too.

The city council race wasn't the only thing that was hot in our room. Maybe somewhere kids learn in air-conditioned comfort, but not in Elmwood Elementary. Our windows got the morning sun, and by afternoon we were inside a furnace. Every day another map or poster fell off the wall as the tape underneath it melted. We were melting, too.

Today when we oozed into our room after recess, all sweaty, dirty, and to tell the truth, smelly, Mrs. Murphy handed out Popsicles. "You all look so hot," she said. "You look like drooping flowers. I can't teach drooping flowers."

She chose a blue one for herself, and we sat with the lights off and a fan blowing over us from the back of the room as we turned our tongues into a rainbow of colors.

It was the sort of moment you wish could last forever, or at least for the five remaining days of school. But, of course, it didn't.

Mrs. Murphy picked up her can of name sticks and shook it. There's a stick for every kid in our class. It's how she picks us for teams, or to answer questions, or whatever. "I'm going to choose partners for one last social studies project," she said.

The class got so quiet, all you could hear was the hum of the fan. We were all waiting to find out if this was one of her good projects, like acting out the Boston Tea Party, or one that was worth moaning about.

"We're going to put on a news show," she said. "One of you will be a famous person in history, and the other will be the TV interviewer. This afternoon we'll go to the library, where you will research your person and write questions and answers together. Tomorrow you'll present your project to the class, just as if you were on TV."

At least it didn't sound like homework would be part of it. And our library (thank you, thank you, thank you) is air-conditioned.

Mrs. Murphy started drawing names. "Caitlin Bishop," she said. "And Eric Clark."

Caitlin? I had to work with Caitlin? I took one look at her and saw she was thinking the same thing. We glared at each other. Then I started thinking of all sorts of possibilities. Hitler. John Wilkes Booth. Any rotten person in history would suit her just fine.

In the library, Caitlin didn't waste any time getting down to business. She's the kind of student who loves to have her report done before the teacher even assigns it. But when I found out what she had in mind, I exploded.

"What?" I shouted. "That's the stupidest thing I ever heard!" Even the air conditioning in the library couldn't keep me cool this time.

Caitlin didn't look very cool herself. She had bright pink circles on her cheeks. "Eric Clark!" she sputtered. "You wouldn't know a good idea if it bit you on your nose!"

"Since when is interviewing the 'historical person' Roger Bishop a good idea?" I stormed.

"Hey, cool it, you guys," said Jonathan. "You don't want Mrs. Murphy coming over here."

Jonathan and his partner, Jessica, had staked out the other half of our table for working on their project. It seemed to me that they were sitting closer together than they needed to. And Jessica was nodding at every brilliant thing Jon said.

"It just so happens I would like Mrs. Murphy to come over here," I said. "Maybe she can explain

"You wouldn't know a good idea if it bit you
on your nose!"

to my so-called partner that her uncle is NOT a famous person in history!"

I had done it now. Mrs. Murphy was on her way.

"Mrs. Murphy," I said, "would you please tell Caitlin that her uncle, even though he's the mayor," I said, pausing to bow at the mere mention of his name, "is not a famous person in history?"

Mrs. Murphy looked thoughtful.

"But look at Eric's list of suggestions," said Caitlin. "Hitler, John Wilkes Booth, Attila the Hun." She made a face that made you think she had just licked a skunk. "I think we should choose someone who has tried to make the world, or at least his town, a better place."

I really hated Caitlin when she started sounding like a nice person. I crossed my arms and slouched down in my seat.

Mrs. Murphy said, "You know what to do when a group has a problem choosing. It's June, for heaven's sake." She raised her eyebrow, waiting.

I sighed. "Pick a number, Jonathan."

Jonathan sat up so fast he almost bumped heads with Jessica. "Go ahead," he said.

I picked first. "One." I knew he'd pick his birthday, and I've gone to his New Year's Day birthday party since we were in kindergarten.

"Seven," said Caitlin.

"Seven it is," said Jonathan, and just like that went back to impressing Jessica.

I sat there, stunned. I started wondering why he let Caitlin win. He could have said I won. Didn't he even care that I was sitting here with my arch enemy? And now I had to write an interview about someone my mom was spending my vacation money trying to beat!

"Oh yeah, he's real smart," I said to Jessica.

She looked up at me in surprise.

Everything that had ever bugged me about Jonathan just started popping up like bubbles in boiling water.

"He reads the encyclopedia for fun. He always has to be the winner when we play chess. And he never stops to think about being fair." In the back of my mind the thought crept in that I was mad at him for the very reason that he had been fair in letting Caitlin win. I swept the thought away as fast as I could. "He even cheats when he plays Candyland!" I didn't say that he cheated to let his little sister win. "Come on, Caitlin," I said. "Let's go work at a different table."

By the time we found a place to spread out our papers, it was almost time to go.

"Look," Caitlin said quietly. "I could just write up the questions and answers, and then all you have to do is read your part."

I stared at her with what I hoped was stony silence.

"Eric," she said, "he's a really good person."

Maybe. But when I left school that afternoon, that really good person was staring out from the IN THE NEWS bulletin board with an eye patch, a Hitler mustache, and fangs.

I didn't sit by Jonathan on the bus. I was still mad at him for what had happened in the library. He didn't seem to care. He sat with Tyler.

When we got off the bus, I walked away without speaking. The day was hot, and the dust kicked up by the bus hung in the air. As I passed Lenox Field, I saw a machine bite a chunk out of the earth and dump it into a waiting truck. I figured it was just a matter of time before there was nothing left of my Lenox Field—not even a rock or a blade of grass. All because of Roger Bishop. The same Roger Bishop I now had to do a report on, all because of Jonathan.

I heard footsteps behind me. I knew it was Jon, but I didn't turn around.

"I don't know why I ever helped you," he said. "All this election business was for nothing. This park's history." He turned away at the next corner without another word.

I didn't try to stop him. I was too hot to explain everything Mom had done—the meetings, the phone calls. Jon knew all that, anyway. He knew she had pushed for a better park than the Ash Tray, I mean Ash Street one that the council had offered. She was pretty sure they were going to agree to it, too.

I pulled a water bottle out of my backpack and poured some over my head and down my throat. I crisscrossed the street from tree shadow to tree shadow. I was grateful for the dark coolness inside our house when I finally got home. The light on our answering machine was flashing. I pushed the button to see who had called.

"Hello, Mrs. Clark," the voice said.

I knew that voice. It was the voice of doom.

"This is Mrs. Murphy," the voice continued. "Please give me a call." She gave her number, and the machine clicked to a stop.

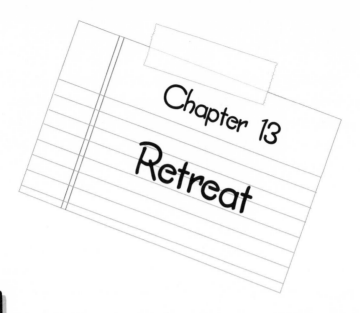

Chapter 13
Retreat

I got it from both sides at dinner. First my mom, then my dad, then my mom, and on and on. Honestly, I don't know how they found the time to eat. If Mrs. Murphy asked me to write a five-page paper tomorrow about honor and playing fair and getting along well with others, I could do it, having just heard about one thousand, ninety-nine examples.

Actually, that sounded like something Mrs. Murphy might just tell me to do, considering the circumstances. I swallowed my milk with a gulp.

". . . and Mrs. Murphy expects you to make an apology to Caitlin tomorrow in front of the class," Mom said.

"O.K.," I said. I wasn't sure if that was a better or worse deal than a five-page report, but I was in no position to bargain.

"Just remember, Eric," Mom said. "If I am elected to city council, I may very well have to work with Roger Bishop. Do you think the city council could get any work done if they spent all their time arguing? Or worse, not even speaking to each other?"

"But if you don't agree on something, if you think it's wrong, you can't just go along with it," I said.

"It's O.K. to disagree. But if people want to accomplish anything, they need to find common ground. They need to find little things they agree on. They have to be willing to listen to other people's ideas."

I just sat there. I didn't like what I was hearing.

Dad spoke up. "Tomorrow, Mrs. Murphy said you and Caitlin have a project to finish up. I expect you to listen to her. No arguments, not this time. I want you to try to see her point of view. Why does she think that way?"

Because she's an idiot, I wanted to say, but I knew that was a sure way to be grounded the rest of my life, so I just said, "O.K., Dad."

I had to wash the dishes and take out the garbage, which was O.K., I guess, since I couldn't watch any TV or play any video games. The phone rang once, but I heard my dad say, "I'm sorry, Eric can't talk to you tonight." This was the most trouble I had been in since Jonathan and I tried making green Jell-O in his little sister's wading pool.

I thought back to the picture of Mr. Bishop with the eye patch and mustache. It had seemed so funny at the time. Now I didn't feel like smiling in the least.

The next morning at school, it was pledge to the flag and morning announcements followed by Eric Clark faces the class. I had my speech all written out on a card so I wouldn't be tempted to add anything funny.

"I, Eric Clark, admit I was wrong. I drew on Roger Bishop's picture. (He looks better in a mustache, I wanted to add.) People need to work together, not tear each other down, especially in government. Caitlin, I'm sorry." (That was part of the deal—I had to call her by name and say I was sorry.)

I went back to my seat. Caitlin didn't say a word. Nobody said a word. I looked at Jonathan, but he just stared over my head at the clock on the wall, like it was really interesting.

After recess (which I, of course, did not get) we went back to the library to finish up our reports. I sat about as far away from Caitlin as I could and still be at the same table. She handed me a blue folder. She held a matching one. "Roger Bishop," it said on the cover. I flipped mine open. There was page after page, perfectly typed.

"What did you do, have your personal secretary type this up for you?" I said. It was so like Caitlin to go overboard like this. Everybody else's report was scrawled out on notebook paper.

Caitlin's cheeks turned pink. "My mom, it just so happens, thought my idea was wonderful, so she invited Uncle Roger to come over. I asked him questions, and she typed up what we said. Look, all you have to do is read your part. You're Roger Bishop, and I'm the reporter."

"Oh no, Caitlin," I said, trying to disagree in that polite way Mom and Dad had told me about. "Roger's your uncle. You should be Roger. In fact, I'd think you'd want to be Roger." I really did not want to be the person I hated so much. I mean, disliked.

It didn't work. Caitlin looked at me like I was crazy. "I'm a girl. You're a boy. My uncle's a man," she said. "Figure it out."

I was going to have to spend some time feeling sorry for my mom if she ended up on city council trying to work together with Caitlin's uncle, if he was anything like her. I sighed and flipped open my folder.

"Do you want to practice together?" she asked.

"Ah, thank you, no. I'll just sit here quietly and read it to myself," I said. But I didn't read it at all. I just sat there playing with the letters in Roger Bishop's name. ROGER: Really Ornery Guy Eats Rats. BISHOP: Big Industrialist Steals Homeless Orphan's Pillow.

Then Mrs. Murphy stood up. "Time's up," she announced. "Let's start our program."

I hadn't read a single word.

Of course Mrs. Murphy picked us to go first. Caitlin was ready. She smiled like there was some imaginary camera only she could see.

"Welcome to our show," she said. "We are fortunate to have with us today a famous war hero, winner of our city's Golden Neighbor award, and five-time city council member. Please join me in welcoming Mr. Roger Bishop."

The class applauded.

War hero? I thought. Did she make that up?

"Tell me, Mr. Bishop," she said. She paused. She gave my foot a little kick.

I looked down at my page. "Um, please call me Roger," I said, reading my part. Please call me Roger? This is going to kill me. Any minute now my heart is going to stop beating.

"All right, then, Roger." Caitlin smiled. "Why don't you start by telling us about your childhood."

Childhood? How long was this interview going to be?

Caitlin kicked my foot again.

"Well, Caitlin, I was born and raised right here in this city, played halfback on the high-school football team. I was the captain. I wanted to go to college, but two months before graduation, my dad lost his job."

The room was so quiet I could hear the clock ticking.

"After graduation I spent the whole summer looking for a job to help out my family. There weren't many businesses or factories in town back then, and the ones that were here weren't hiring."

"What did you do?" Caitlin asked.

I turned the page. "I decided to join the Army. It seemed like the only way I was going to get an education and a good job. There was just one problem."

"What was that?"

"There was a war going on halfway around the world in Vietnam."

"Is that where you became a war hero?"

"It didn't seem like being a hero at the time. It just seemed like trying to stay alive, and trying to keep my buddies alive."

"What happened?" Caitlin asked.

It was eerie. Everybody had these looks on their faces like they were wondering if I was going to live or die. Heck, I was almost wondering if I was going to live or die. I read on.

"It happened so fast. There was a grenade. It blew us out of our jeep. Dirt and rocks were flying everywhere, and smoke and fire. My leg was cut pretty bad, but I was in better shape than some of my buddies. I helped drag two of them back to the base before I blacked out."

"Is that how you lost your leg?"

My leg? I looked down at my leg. Didn't Roger Bishop have two legs? I looked back at my paper.

"That's right, Caitlin," I read. "It was a tough break for a kid who had been running down football fields the year before, let me tell you. I can't win any races with this artificial leg of mine, but after all these years, I've made peace with it."

Mrs. Murphy pointed to her watch. I knew this was taking too long. I looked at Caitlin. She flipped to the last page, and so did I.

"What's your goal for the city, Roger?" Caitlin asked.

I found my place on the page and answered. "My goal has always been to make our city a good place to live and work. Our city council has brought many new businesses to our town over the past few years. This is important. I never want a young man to have such a hard time finding a job in our town that he has to leave. I had to leave once, and I'm thankful I had a chance to come back."

"Thank you, Roger Bishop," Caitlin said, and we were done. Everyone clapped as we shook hands. (It was in the script.) Then we walked back to our seats. People were smiling and nodding at me, as if I really were Roger Bishop, war hero, instead of Eric Clark, eye-patch-and-mustache-drawing jerk.

Chapter 14

Summer

The last few days of school melted away like a Popsicle on a hot sidewalk. My life was kind of a mess like that, too. Caitlin and I were politely not talking, but Jonathan was out-and-out rude.

If I sat at the front of the bus, he sat at the back. If I ran home, he walked. If I walked, he ran. He waited till I sat down for lunch and then picked the table farthest away. The more he avoided me, the more sure I was that I didn't want to have anything to do with him.

Until the first day of summer vacation.

Jonathan goes away every summer because his parents are divorced and he spends his vacation with his dad. Since he's never here for the Fourth of July, we always celebrate it the first night of vacation, before he leaves. Of course, our moms never let us use real fireworks, so we do the next best thing. We pour pixie sticks into bottles of Mountain Dew. Maybe they don't explode, light up, or make any loud noises, but they do make a really cool bubbling landslide. Jon always makes sure to set the bottles on the sidewalk near an anthill. He says it's the best entertainment the ants will have all year, and then to make sure, he does a kind of play-by-play announcement, like it's an erupting-bottle sports event.

Only this year, Jon never came over, and then he was gone.

A few weeks later, I was sitting on the dock, dangling my feet in the water up at the lake on our vacation. Our two-night vacation, I might add. The first day it had rained, and the next day it was too cold and windy to swim.

Dad came out of the cabin carrying my shoes and socks. "Come on. Let's go for a hike," he said.

I led the way through the trees. I started to sing the song Dad had taught me on a hike long ago. "The other day . . ."

Dad sang the echo and added, "I saw a bear," and I knew this was going to be a good walk. Sure enough. We sang every verse we knew, and then Dad started making up goofy ones like, "The other day, I saw a porcupine."

The trail went higher and higher through the woods, and at last we found ourselves looking down at the stream far below. Dad sat down on a log to rest.

"Eric," he said.

It was that serious-sounding "Eric" that usually makes me wonder what I had done. This time, though, I wasn't worried. Maybe it was the humming of the insects or the way the light coming through the trees fell in little patches. Everything seemed too peaceful for me to be in any trouble.

"Eric," he said again. "You are without a doubt an amazing son. I still can't believe you masterminded this election. And you brought your social studies grade up to an A."

Small wonder. I had a little extra credit helping me out.

"And you even brought your work habits grade up to an A."

And that would be because I never ever forgot to bring in my current events homework the rest of the year. Sometimes I even brought in two.

"I'm really proud of you," he said.

This was magic. This was perfect. For a second I felt like I did when I was little and he threw me up into the air and caught me.

"I know you had that little run-in with Caitlin," he went on.

Oh well. I started climbing a tree while he talked. It was one of those inviting kind of trees with low branches that practically pull you up into them before you know what's happened.

Dad looked at me to see if I was listening.

Everything seemed too peaceful for me to be in any trouble.

"But I learned a lot from that," I said. "I learned about having to work with others even if you don't always agree with them."

"Yes, and your mom and I . . ."

I sat on a small branch and flipped over till I was hanging by my knees. Then I heard a *crack*, and so did Dad. He grabbed me and set me down on the ground so hard and fast I could barely catch my breath. And the magic was gone. It was so far gone, it was like it had never happened.

"For crying out loud!" Dad hollered. "I was just about to tell you how responsible you've become, and then you go and do something like that! Sometimes I wonder if you've gained a lick of sense since you were four."

He stomped down the hill, swatting clouds of gnats out of his way.

I knew just how they felt.

And the next day, our vacation ended.

Summer dragged on and on. Mom spent lots of evenings going to meetings or speaking to different groups. Every Saturday afternoon she and Dad were busy going door to door, handing out her pamphlets. I tagged along a couple of times. We met all kinds of people. If somebody knew my mom or dad, we'd stop and talk for a while. That might sound like a good thing, but usually they just ended up talking about somebody's Great-aunt

Edna who got food poisoning from Cousin Mabel's potato salad. We didn't get very far if there were a couple of talkers on a block.

Lots of people just took the pamphlet, mumbled something, and closed the door quick, like they were afraid we might push our way in, sit them down, and talk about Aunt Edna for the next hour or so.

Every so often I'd see one of my VOTE FOR LIZ CLARK signs, especially in yards near old Lenox Field. That was a great feeling. But we saw signs for Roger Bishop, too, and every other candidate. I was a little bit worried about twelve people running for city council. It meant that five of them were going to lose. And six of them were already on the council and wanted to get elected again. Dad said that kind of gave them a head start because people already knew their names. I started counting to see who had the most signs, but Roger Bishop was winning, so I stopped.

"I don't get it," I said to Mom one afternoon as we walked down yet another street. "I thought that Roger Bishop was a bad guy, a park killer. But then Caitlin tells our class he's some kind of hero. Is that true?"

Mom nodded. "It was big news here about thirty years ago."

"And did he really get a lot of businesses to come to our town?"

"I think that would be fair to say."

"So . . ." I tried to find the right words. This had been bugging me since Caitlin and I had done the interview. "Was he right about selling the park and taxes and businesses and all that?"

Mom sighed and smiled half a smile. "I've got a more difficult race ahead of me than I thought if my own son has gone over to the enemy."

"But you said . . ."

"That the city council has to work together and that he's not really an enemy," Mom said. "I know, I was just kidding." She stopped smiling. "Roger Bishop has his good intentions, I suppose, and he loves his city. But not every idea that man has is twenty-four-carat gold, despite his Golden Neighbor award, his medals, and his decade of service on city council. You remember that. Every so often someone else around here might just have an idea better than his. And that person might be somebody's mother!"

I laughed. "And that somebody's mother just might be our next mayor!"

After another day of knocking on doors, I knew I needed something to do, and I needed somebody to do it with. It was time to find a new best friend.

As soon as I got home, I started making a list. I was really getting good at making lists.

NEW BEST FRIEND
1. Must have a good sense of humor.
2. Must be able to invent new games.
3. Must have a good imagination.

I paused. This was a good list. Why hadn't I done this before? Jon didn't really have a sense of humor. How many times had he rolled his eyes at my jokes? And his imagination needed work. True, he was good at inventing new games, I'd give him that. But, I decided, I could do better. I added one more number to my list.

4. Must know what it means to be a real friend.

Unlike Jonathan.

O.K. I had my list. I was ready to audition new best friends. I called Zac. We had done stuff together last summer when Jon was gone. He was fun. Zac had possibilities.

Zac's mother answered the phone. "He's over at Steve's today," she said. "I'll tell him you called."

I called Nick. "Sure, I'll come over," he said. "Just as soon as I finish this level." Nick spent a lot of time playing video games.

Two hours later, he finally showed up. I had been waiting on my front step so long, I think I actually saw the grass grow.

"Come on," I said. "Let's play air baseball." Air baseball was a game Jon had invented and I had improved.

"Is it a video game?" Nick asked.

I shook my head. This wasn't going to be easy.

"So where's your bat and ball?" Nick asked.

"It's air baseball," I said. "You have to use your imagination." I pointed out the imaginary bases in my backyard. "I'll pitch first and show you."

The last time Jon and I had played, it had been the Interplanetary All-Star Game over at Lenox Field. I had been an alien with eight tentacles who threw an awesome sucker ball. This time I decided to try out my new curve ball. "Get ready," I said.

I whirled my right arm around like a windmill, then my left. I spun around two times and released the pitch.

Nick just stood there.

"Strike!" I called.

"What?" said Nick. "What am I supposed to do?"

I tried to be patient. "You hit the ball and run the bases, and you get a home run if I don't tag you out."

Nick narrowed his eyes and studied me like I was mystery meat on the school cafeteria tray.

"Looks like I'm going to have to send you my slider," I said. This time I did a cartwheel, threw the ball, and ended up on my stomach.

"I don't get it," Nick said.

I stood up and dusted myself off. "All right." I sighed. "Video games it is."

I tried Zac again the next day.

"He and Steve went to the city pool," his mother said.

Great. Just great. Obviously Zac was not in the market for a new friend.

I called Tyler and he came right over, bringing his brand-new remote-controlled racecar with him.

"Sweet!" I said. "Let's try it out."

Tyler tried it out. I watched. I barely ever got a turn that lasted more than fifteen seconds.

"I know," I said. "Let's hide behind that tree over there, and when somebody comes along the sidewalk, we'll drive the car right at him. It'll be so funny!"

Tyler looked at me. "Sitting behind that tree doing nothing but waiting for who knows how long is going to be funny?" he asked.

In my head I made a big X over Tyler's name as I crossed him off my list of new best friends.

The day after Tyler I was so desperate for something to do, I decided to go door to door with Mom and Dad again. This time we actually found some people who were interested in what the city council was doing. One man's kids had all played ball at Lenox Field. "You get me a sign, and I'll be happy to put it up in my yard," he said.

At another house a lady asked me, "Aren't you the boy who wrote the letter to the editor about Lenox Field?"

I said I was.

"Charlie, come here," she called. "It's that boy from the newspaper."

I didn't know if that was a good thing or a bad thing, and I tried to think of a good reason why I had to be going. Before I could, a big man in a Power Gym T-shirt came out. I'll tell you, he was about as big as a grizzly bear. I was ready to run for it.

He stuck out his arm. "Let me shake your hand," he said. His voice boomed. "You sure told that city council a few things." He took a pamphlet. "You bet I'll vote for your mom." He slapped me on the back. "I'd vote for you if I could, kid."

After that, I was kind of in a daze for a couple of blocks. All of a sudden I found myself standing in front of Jonathan's house. The flip-flopping my stomach did in front of Mr. Grizzly was nothing compared to the roller-coaster dives it was taking now.

"Uh, Dad? I think I'll go help Mom on the other side of the street," I said.

"Don't be silly," Dad said. "This is your friend Jonathan's house. We should stop and say hello and thank his mother again for helping with the petitions."

That would be a great plan if her son wasn't mad at me, but what could I say?

Mrs. Pierce came to the door and smiled at me. "Well, hello, Eric," she said. "I sure do miss seeing you when Jonathan's away."

My dad shook her hand, and they started talking about the city council.

Whew, I thought. Jonathan must not have told his mom about what a jerk I'd been. Maybe he hadn't told her because he'd been kind of a jerk, too. All of a sudden I really needed to see Jon again. Summer was just too boring without him.

"When's Jon coming home, Mrs. Pierce?" I asked.

"The first of August," she said. "I'll have him call you after I get enough hugs out of him."

August first came and went with no sign of Jonathan. But the next day the phone rang. I grabbed it.

"Mom told me to call you."

It was Jonathan. He didn't sound too excited about seeing me.

"Come on over, Jon," I said. "A whole summer's long enough to be mad at me. Let's do something."

"Well . . ."

"We could go over and see how they're fixing up the new park they're making us," I said.

"The new park they're making us?" he repeated. "It sounds like they're making it just for you and me."

"Well, of course they are," I said. "They're going to have this huge sign, too—the Eric and Jonathan City Park."

"You mean the Jonathan and Eric City Park," Jon said.

"Only if you change the order of the alphabet, buddy," I said. "E before J. Bring your bike. I don't think I could stand to walk that far."

It took us a while to get there, even on our bikes. There wasn't much grass yet, and it didn't have a baseball field, but there was a brand-new climb-and-slide sort of play thing over in one corner.

Jonathan climbed on it and hung by his knees. "So where's the sign?" he asked. "The big Jonathan and Eric sign?"

"They sent it back because it was too small. They wanted to make it even big—"

That's when I noticed the sign. It was right behind the monkey bars, facing the road. Jon and I walked around it slowly, like two wolves circling their prey.

"Oh no!" I cried.

ROGER BISHOP PARK, the sign declared.

"That's hardly fair," Jonathan said. "Roger Bishop only decided to build this park because your mom got everybody all upset about turning Lenox Field into a bunch of houses. It should be the Liz Clark Park."

I looked at Jon. "Does this mean that you're not mad at me anymore?"

"Mad at you? I was only mad at you because you were mad at me!" he said.

"Mad at you?" I said. "I was mad at Caitlin, not you."

Jonathan and I looked at each other, shaking our heads. "So how come two people who weren't really mad at each other managed to miss out on their annual, pre-Fourth-of-July erupting soda-pop volcano?" he asked.

I smiled. "It just so happens that I still have the pixie sticks I bought last June ready and waiting."

"I'll bring the soda," Jonathan volunteered.

We grabbed our bikes and started for home, but not before I took a piece of paper out of my pocket and hung it on the sign. It was great. Right under the words Roger Bishop Park, it said, VOTE FOR LIZ CLARK.

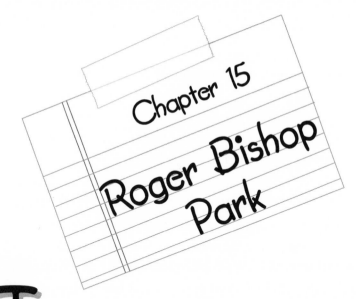

Chapter 15
Roger Bishop Park

The funny thing about summer is that no matter how it drags in the middle, it goes by way too fast at the end. One day you're running through the sprinkler in bare feet, and the next day you're stuffing those feet into stiff new shoes and loading new pens and notebooks into your backpack. Going into sixth grade meant going to a bigger school with more kids. The good thing about the new school year was that Caitlin, finally, wasn't in my class. The bad thing was, neither was Jonathan.

At least Jon and I got to see each other at lunch. We sat together and ignored the fact that Caitlin was there, too. At least I ignored her until the third week of school, when her uncle Roger walked into the cafeteria carrying two bags of hamburgers, fries, and milk shakes. Let me repeat that: Hamburgers! Fries! Shakes! Then he sat down with Caitlin at our table, handed her one of the bags, and they started eating. At our table!

The agonizing smell of French fries drifted straight down our way. I looked at my peanut butter sandwich in disgust. Do you know how long it's been since I had a single French fry? Since May! My mom and dad weren't kidding when they said we were going to cut back on eating out. And now Roger Bishop, the man responsible for my fast-food starvation, was sitting not three feet away from me, gobbling down one golden fry after another. I thought about breaking off pieces of my sandwich, wadding them into little bread balls, and firing them in his direction, but Jon grabbed my arm.

"Come on," he said. "Let's get out of here."

Outside on the playground I said, "I can't believe her uncle brought her a Happy Value meal. Why did it have to be her uncle?"

"Didn't I tell you?" Jonathan asked. "He's talking to our class after lunch."

Oh, was I ever happy I wasn't in that class. I know I would have made a VOTE FOR LIZ CLARK sign, taped it to my ruler, and held it up in protest while he was speaking. And I would have been in detention for about a month.

I made a face. "He never came to talk at our school any other year," I said. "I bet Caitlin asked him just to annoy me."

Jessica joined us. She spoke up. "Actually, I think

he came because he's worried about the election this time. I overheard Caitlin's mom talking to my mom about it."

I stared at Jessica. My mouth must have been hanging open, because Jessica started laughing.

"Why are you staring?" Jon asked. "You know Jessica and Caitlin are neighbors."

Yes, of course. Jessica and Caitlin are neighbors. And Jonathan and Jessica are friends. And, thank my lucky stars, Jonathan and I are friends again.

"That look in your eye," said Jessica. "What is it?"

I rubbed my hands together and smiled an evil smile. "Jessica," I said. "Dear, dear Jessica. How would you like to be a spy?"

Jessica rolled her eyes. "What's there to spy on? He shakes people's hands and says, 'Vote for me.' He talks at schools and clubs."

"He gets his picture in the newspaper," added Jonathan. He pointed across the parking lot at the *Daily Herald* news van. Out climbed a bald man with a serious camera.

I groaned. "This man must be stopped!"

"The photographer?" Jessica asked.

"No," I said. "Roger Bishop! Maybe what we need is our own photographer. Someone who could take a picture that shows the real Roger Bishop." I wondered if I had any film left in my camera at home.

"Jessica," I said, grabbing her shoulders. "You've got to find out where Caitlin's uncle lives!"

"He lives across from the new Roger Bishop Park," Jessica said. "I thought everybody knew that. My dad says it must be nice to be so important you can get taxpayers to build a park right across the street from your house and name it after you."

I was in shock. "My mom pushed to have a park put in across the street from Roger Bishop's house?" No wonder there was all that whispering going on at the council meeting when she suggested it.

"Don't feel bad," Jessica said. "My dad said he's just happy it didn't get turned into the mayor's own private tennis court and putting green."

I was still steamed. "Why hasn't the newspaper printed anything about this?" I asked.

Jonathan pointed to Roger Bishop. His one arm was around Caitlin's shoulder. The other one was busy pumping the bald man's hand. "I'd say he's got the newspaper in his pocket," he said.

I started spending a lot of time at the Vote for Liz Clark Field. (I just couldn't call it Roger Bishop Park.) Sometimes I went with Jonathan, and sometimes it was just me and my camera.

A month went by. The leaves turned from green to red and gold. Now there was less than a month left until the election. The problem was, Roger Bishop was almost never home. And when he was, he was doing something nice, like carrying out the garbage for the old lady who lived next-door. Or tossing a baseball to some neighbor kids. He was pretty strong for a guy with only one real leg. Why did he have to be so nice?

I knew it had to be an act. I bet when nobody was watching, he probably kicked his dog or stole his neighbor's newspaper. I had to find out.

The very next Saturday was warm and sunny. I got to the park early in the morning and climbed the big willow tree by the street, just across from Roger Bishop's house. I was prepared to wait. I had a bag of grapes, some pretzels, a water bottle, and of course, my camera.

In the first hour, fourteen different people jogged by or walked by or rode a bike or pushed a stroller by. The fifteenth person was a little old lady walking a little wiry dog. All of a sudden the dog started yipping like a wind-up toy. He strained at his leash. And he was looking right up at me!

"Boo-Boo," the lady called. "Stop that. Be a good doggie."

Boo-Boo growled.

"Boo-Boo, what is wrong with you?" she said, tugging on his leash.

I threw a grape at him, trying to get his attention away from me.

At the same moment, Roger Bishop stepped out his front door to get his morning paper and looked over to see what all the commotion was about. He was wearing pajama bottoms and a sleeveless undershirt. Roger Bishop in his pajamas was hardly Roger Bishop kicking a dog, but I was desperate. I reached for my camera, but it slipped from my fingers. I lunged for it and knew immediately that I had made a big, big mistake. I found myself falling through the air, with grapes flying around me like green hail.

I hit the ground too fast and too hard to scream. All the wind was knocked right out of me. It didn't matter, though, because the little old lady did enough screaming for both of us, with Boo-Boo adding his barks like exclamation marks.

I tried to sit up, but my right leg was twisted under me in a funny way, and all of a sudden I noticed how much it hurt. And I mean hurt! I hate to admit it, but I started to cry.

The next minute, there was Roger Bishop, pajamas and all, bending over me.

"Just lie still, son. Help is on the way. Do you want me to give your mom a call?" he asked.

I gave him my number.

"What's your mom's name?" he asked.

This surprised me. I thought he'd never forget me after that first council meeting. Maybe he thinks all kids look alike.

"What's her name, son?" he repeated.

If my leg hadn't hurt so bad, I might really have enjoyed the look on his face when I answered.

"Liz Clark," I said.

I found myself falling . . . .

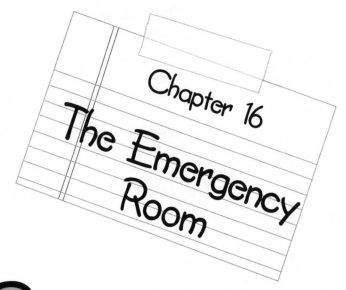

Chapter 16
The Emergency Room

Roger Bishop stayed right there by me, waiting for the ambulance. He picked up my water bottle and bag of pretzels and put them next to me. Boo-Boo got a couple of the grapes before Little Old Lady dragged him away. Mr. Bishop held up my camera.

"I'm afraid your camera is broken," he said. He was silent for a moment, and then he asked, "Just what were you doing up in that tree?"

How could I tell this man in pajamas, who had just called the ambulance and my mom, that I was spying on him? And taking his picture in those very pajamas?

I cleared my throat. "I was trying to take some pictures of birds," I said. It was a lie, of course, and it burned in my throat and on my tongue. But what else could I say? "I saw a black one with orange on his wings the other day when I was playing here in the park," I added. At least that part was true.

"Hmm," said Mr. Bishop.

I tried to imagine what my mother was going to say. I thought about it all the way to the hospital.

When the ambulance guys wheeled me into emergency, I lifted my head off the stretcher, searching for her face. I wanted to see what kind of look she had in her eyes. Was it going to be a thank-heavens-he's-alive-look or an Eric-you've-really-blown-it-this-time look? I was so busy searching for her wavy gold hair that at first I looked right past him.

My dad.

"Eric," he said.

Sometimes my dad's face is hard to read, but not this time. His face looked gray, and his eyes were streaked with tiny pink lines. His arms hung loose at his sides. He had on a plaid flannel shirt with tiny pinholes burnt through the sleeves. I knew he had been working on his animal sculptures again, welding them together with his torch. He looked kind of like he needed to be welded back together himself.

"Eric," he said again, and he reached out to put his hand on my shoulder, looking first to the hospital guy to make sure it was O.K. to touch me. Then he shook his head. Not that disappointed shake I know so well, but more of a trying-to-wake-up-from-a-bad-dream shake. "What were you doing up in a tree?" he asked.

"I was stupid. It was a stupid idea." I hadn't planned to say that. The words just fell out of my mouth on their own.

Dad nodded. He started to relax. For some reason, I think parents enjoy hearing their kids admit they made a mistake.

They put us in a little curtained-off room, bare except for shelves and drawers and a single plastic chair. The only picture on the wall was a row of faces, from smiling to crying, labeled, "How Much Does It Hurt?" I guessed it was for little kids who couldn't find the words to say, "It feels like a rabid beaver is chewing on my leg bone!" Which happened to describe exactly how I was feeling at the moment.

Dad looked around. "Not much has changed since last time."

"You mean when I broke my collarbone?" I asked. I thought back. "I must have been about four," I said.

"Two weeks after your fifth birthday," Dad said. He stared into the distance. "Such a beautiful spring day. Mom was working."

"Doing taxes," I guessed.

"And we were having the greatest time." He pulled the plastic chair over but didn't sit down. "We played on every swing, every slide."

"And we hunted for aliens in the woods," I said, suddenly remembering. "You said the mushrooms were little miniature flying saucers." I smiled in spite of the rabid beaver.

But Dad wasn't smiling. He slowly sank into the chair. "It was my fault," he said. "'Into the spaceship! They're after us!' That's what I said. And you ran up the steps of that slide. You were laughing and shrieking. You stood there at the very top, and I shouted, 'They're coming! Quick! Into the worm hole!' and you turned and lost your balance and . . ."

". . . and I fell."

"And you're still falling in parks and breaking bones," Dad said. He shook his head again, a disappointed shake this time. But I had the feeling he was disappointed in himself.

I hated to see him so worried. "It was an accident," I said. "Accidents happen."

"Try telling that to your mother during tax time," he said.

And just like that, I could see the two of them crowded into a tiny room like this. I imagined Mom flying out of her office, leaving behind a waiting room full of people. No, Mom doesn't believe in accidents. She believes in planning and list making and being on time. Imaginary aliens are not a big part of her life. My parents had argued in whispers in this emergency room. And Dad and I never went to the park again.

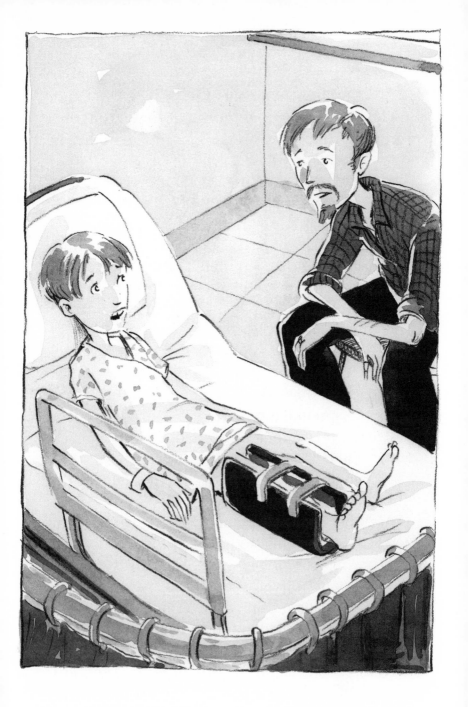

"Your mother," he said, "will not laugh."

"At least I wasn't running away from aliens this time," I said. "I was doing it all for Mom." I found myself pouring out the whole story, from Caitlin's uncle bringing hamburgers to school and getting photographed to Boo-Boo chasing my falling grapes. Dad could hardly believe me at first, but by the time I got to Boo-Boo he was laughing. He pulled out his bandanna to wipe his eyes.

Dad cleared his throat and became serious. "Your mother," he said, "will not laugh."

"I know," I said, "but I'd better tell her. She'll never believe I was taking pictures of birds anyhow."

Mom didn't laugh. But she didn't lecture either. She must have been glad to see us after all the hours we spent in the emergency room. She gave me a hug, listened to my story, and gave me a hug again. Then she took a black Magic Marker and wrote "MOM" on my cast. I took the marker next and added the words, "FOR MAYOR."

She almost laughed then, but rolled her eyes and said, "The lengths to which some people will go to try to get a vote!"

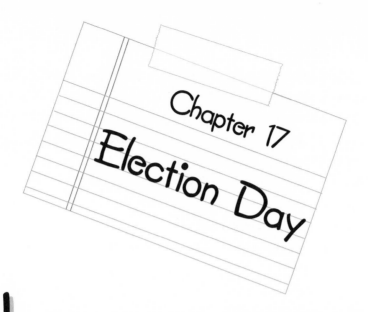

Chapter 17
Election Day

woke up to the sound of my dad whistling down in the kitchen even before my alarm went off. Election day! I raced to the kitchen. Well, really, with my leg in a cast, it was more like hobbling.

Dad stood at the stove, spatula in hand. "I'm making lucky pancakes this morning," he said. He poured the batter carefully into the sizzling pan, making a zigzag shape. "W—for win," he explained.

I took the handle of the pan and gave it a turn. "M—for mayor," I said.

"Or V—for victory," he said with a laugh when a pancake broke apart as he slid it onto my plate.

"I think I'm too nervous to eat," Mom said when she came in. She had on a sweatshirt and tennis shoes—definitely not office clothes. I knew she was planning to go to voting places, stand across the parking lot with a sign, and wave at all the people who came to vote. I was desperate to get out of school to come and help.

"Let me come with you today, Mom, please?" I begged. I was pretty sure it was hopeless, because we'd been through this before, but it was worth a try. "I won't be able to concentrate at school today anyway."

Mom poured herself a cup of coffee. "Make sure you have your key," she said. "Jon's mom said she'd give you a ride home after school. Dad and I will be home between six and seven. Aunt Debby's coming over later to listen to the returns. Now go get ready, and I'll give you a ride."

Mom and Dad have been driving me to school since I broke my leg. It's nice, especially when it's raining or cold. But it means I don't get to see Jon till just before third hour when he's running out of Mr. Duncan's English class and I'm running into it.

He met me at the classroom door. "Look at this!" he said. He handed me a picture of a house. It looked like an ad, with a list of stuff like rooms and sizes.

I looked up at the title on the page. *Lenox Housing Development.* Suddenly, all the V and W and M pancakes I had eaten were turning to lead and spelling out Very Wretched Moment. "Where did you get this?" I asked.

"I saw it on Mr. Duncan's desk. I asked him if I could borrow it. He said he's thinking of buying a townhouse there when he retires. It looks pretty cool. There's going to be a community swimming pool, and a walking trail, and . . ."

"You don't have to sound so happy about it," I snapped.

"Eric," Jon said quietly. "The park is gone."

Of course the park was gone. Hadn't I watched the bulldozers plow down the swing set and the monkey bars? Hadn't I watched them uproot tree after tree? Hadn't I seen the little wooden skeleton of the first house just this morning on the drive to school? But somehow I hoped, deep in my heart, that nobody would buy a single one of these houses. Nobody.

The bell sounded, and Jon ran down the hall.

I hobbled into class and slid behind my desk. Mr. Duncan was already passing out our journals. I couldn't even look at him.

"This will be a free writing period," Mr. Duncan announced. "Write on a topic of your choice. Remember to use the elements we've discussed—examples, sensory details, an opening that grabs the reader, and a good conclusion."

Oh, I had a topic all right, and plenty of sensory details. I just had to come up with the perfect opening.

I stared at my blank paper. I tapped my pencil. I wanted to blast the Lenox Housing Development. I wanted to shame Mr. Duncan for even thinking about buying a place there. But I knew I had to sound reasonable. Logical.

I started doodling as I thought. One tree, then another. A woods. Pretty soon aliens were hiding in the branches and spies lurked behind the trunks. I was really getting into this when the bell rang.

"Pass your journals to the front," Mr. Duncan said.

The girl behind me gave me a poke in the back. It kind of woke me up. I was in trouble. Mr. Duncan is not the kind of teacher who would have a sense of humor about drawing spies and aliens instead of writing. But if I didn't turn in any writing, I'd get a zero. I absolutely didn't want to get a zero.

I felt a harder poke. I turned and reached for the pile of notebooks. Then I quickly tore the page out of my journal, folded it up, and stuffed it into my pocket.

The rest of the day at school, all I could think about was that stupid zero. Would Mr. Duncan call my parents and complain about my attitude? He looked like the kind of teacher who might. Report cards were coming out next week, and then parent conferences.

Rats! Things had been going so well. I was using my new list-making skills to organize my school work. My grades were decent. And Dad was whistling. He was singing silly songs. We were having fun again.

"Tell your mom I don't need a ride home after all," I said to Jon at the end of the day. I'd decided I had to find Mom and Dad before they heard from Mr. Duncan.

I went out to the bus loop. Getting my broken leg up the three bus steps took a little doing, but I managed. My family votes at Elmwood Elementary, and I was hoping that's where Mom would be. It was one of my bus's stops. I looked for her sign when our bus pulled up, but all I saw was a pickup truck with a huge Roger Bishop sign in the back. My heart sank. There was nothing to do but go home.

I got off at my regular stop. A big sign announced Lenox Estates Housing Development. Now paved streets complete with curbs twisted through the field. Workmen in heavy coats hammered shingles on the roof of the model home. I started walking around, ignoring how cold my toes at the end of my cast were feeling, even through Dad's thick wool sock.

The grass here was gone—all gone. Sand and gravel covered the whole area. I tried to remember where the slide had been, and the monkey bars. At least they had saved a lot of the trees. I recognized the spot where my path through the woods had started. Maybe the walking trail Jon had mentioned would go through here. I wondered if kids would still be able to play in these woods—or what was left of them.

Just when I was starting to feel good for the first time since breakfast, I tripped over a root. *Oomph!* I fell flat on my stomach. And my face. I wiped the dirt off and saw blood on my hand. My nose was bleeding! I had to roll over to one side and push myself up. Getting up with a leg in a cast is not the easiest thing in the world. It was a long walk back to the sidewalk, and it was going to be an even longer walk home.

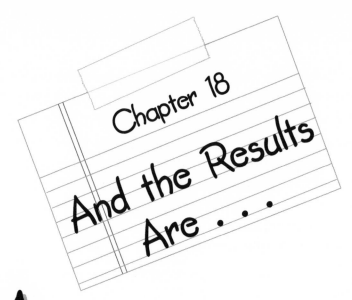

Chapter 18
And the Results Are . . .

A car pulled up behind me, and the engine stopped. I heard the door open and then slam shut.

"Eric!"

It was Mom. I tried to smile, but I was too miserable. I waved a bloody hand.

"I knew as soon as Jon's mom told me you didn't want a ride home there was trouble," she said, but she said it in a soft voice, not a mad one. She pulled some tissues out of her coat pocket and gently cleaned off my face.

"I wanted to find you," I said, trying to explain. "I thought you'd be at Elmwood so I took the bus, but you weren't there, so then all I could do was go home, and then I tripped. . . ." My voice started to crack, and Mom grabbed me in a hug that practically smothered me in her coat.

"Well, you found me," she said. "Now let's get you home."

I couldn't exactly tell my mom about the zero while I was pinching my nostrils together. It would just have to wait.

Once we were home, Mom made me a couple of sandwiches and made sure I was all right.

"I'm going back out for a little while," she said. "A lot of people stop and vote on the way home from work. We're at the high school, though, not Elmwood. I'll have my cell phone on if you need me."

I hardly had time to feel sorry for myself being stuck at home alone. Before I knew it, Aunt Debby was there with bags of groceries. She put me right to work.

"Wow! This is like a party," I said, pulling out pizzas and chips.

"You bet it is," said Aunt Debby.

It wasn't long before Mom and Dad came back, along with some of their friends. Dad turned the radio up loud. We all listened to hear how many votes Mom was getting.

It was scary. Right from the start, Roger Bishop was ahead of everybody, but Mom was picking up a few votes, too. One minute Mom was in 7th place, and the next she was in 8th. Then she'd be back in 7th again. Win, lose, win, lose—it was like a Ping-Pong ball bouncing back and forth. I gave up hoping Mom would finish in first place and be our next mayor. Now I was just desperate for her to finish in the top seven so she could be on the council at all.

Then, in the middle of everything, I heard the worst words.

"Time for bed."

I stared at my mom with my oh-please-no-you've-got-to-be-kidding face, but it didn't do any good.

"It's ten o'clock," she said.

At least she let me keep my radio on. There was no way I'd ever get to sleep, I thought, but the next thing I knew I woke up to the sounds of cheers coming from downstairs. Mom made it! She was going to be on city council! What a bad time to have my leg in a cast. I so wanted to jump up and down on my bed!

It was all right, though, because everybody came into my room and there was more than enough jumping going on. Aunt Debby was dancing. Dancing!

"Enough!" Mom finally said, laughing. "This boy needs his sleep." And she shooed everybody out of my room.

"Wait, Mom, Dad," I said. "There's something I've got to tell you."

Mom sat down next to me, and Dad stood beside her.

Aunt Debby was dancing!

"Jon found a pamphlet on Mr. Duncan's desk this morning," I said. "For the new condos at Lenox Field."

"Ah." Something about mom's voice told me she would understand.

I went on. "And then in English, Mr. Duncan told us to write about a topic of our choice. With examples."

"O.K. You were upset," Dad said. "What did you write?"

"That's the thing," I said. "I didn't. I started drawing a picture, trying to think of what to say. And then the hour was over. I couldn't hand in a picture." I sighed. "So I tore it out of my journal and put it in my pocket."

My parents were silent.

I had to go on. "But the bad news is, I'll get a zero because I didn't turn it in. A zero. And I was afraid you'd be upset." I wanted to add, "And you've just started acting like you're proud of me once in a while," but I didn't.

My dad cleared his throat. "You know what I think about doodling on your school papers," he said. "And now you can see why."

I sighed.

Dad continued. "But I want to say, I think you're quite a young man, Eric, quite a young man. I've been proud of you so many times in the past few months, I've lost count. You got this whole election thing going, and you saw it through right till the end, even after your park was gone. But now, you know, you're going to have to pay for what you've done."

I started to worry, but then I saw him wink.

Dad said, "When Mom has meetings, you're going to have to eat my cooking!"

I went to sleep that night dreaming about what people would say the next day at school.

What a letdown. I found myself missing Mrs. Murphy. Sixth grade social studies is all about Mexico and Canada and South America. No current events. No IN THE NEWS bulletin board. And Mr. Arnett taught straight from the book. I think Jon and Jessica were the only kids in the whole school who even knew there had been an election. Well, except for Caitlin, of course.

At least Jon was excited.

"So do you think your mom can rename the new park the Jon and Eric Park?" he asked me at lunch.

"Eric and Jon Park," I corrected him. "But don't look for it to happen this week." I nodded over toward the next table, where Caitlin was surrounded by her friends. "Roger Bishop is still mayor."

Caitlin looked up. At least she knew about the election. And she was surely informing everyone within the sound of her voice about it. She looked my way and gave me a thumbs-up.

It was weird. After all these months of being enemies, it was like now we were on the same team. I was sorry Caitlin wasn't in my social studies class this year. I'm sure she would have worked the city council election into Mexican history somehow.

I lifted my thumb up in the air, and I held it high.

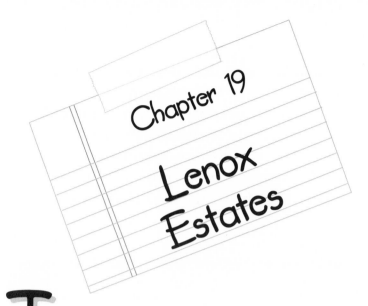

Chapter 19

Lenox Estates

The snow crunched under our feet as Dad and I walked along together.

"It's coming down pretty steady," Dad said as we passed a street lamp. Flakes swirled around us in a triangle of light.

"Do you think the snow will be too deep for us to go through the woods?" I asked. Dad and I had gotten in the habit of taking walks together after dinner when Mom had her meetings. Most of the time, we ended up walking through the little bit of woods they left standing at Lenox Field.

"Just pick up your feet so you don't trip over anything," Dad warned.

The trees were too few and far apart to make the woods really scary anymore, even at night. You could see lights from the street and some of the finished houses no matter where you stood. Dad said

131

that one of these days they were going to pave our trail and paint a line down the middle of it. It just wasn't possible to imagine aliens here these days, or even spies. Sometimes things change.

I glanced over at my dad. He looked at me and grinned. Then opened his mouth and began to sing in a voice that shook the branches. *"On top of spaghetti . . ."*

I had to laugh, and then I had to sing along. Sometime things change, that's true. Still, every once in a while, something changes back.

Author's Note

The city council election in Eric's town in *Mom for Mayor* is based on the system we have in place in my hometown of Port Huron, Michigan. We vote for seven council members, and the council then chooses the top vote-getter to be the mayor. The position of mayor in Port Huron is largely ceremonial. The mayor keeps his or her day job, whatever it may be, as do the council members. The city council hires a city manager to handle the day-to-day operations of the city.

In the towns and cities around me, however, local governments are organized differently. Some cities elect a mayor to a full-time, paid position rather than hiring a city manager. Other towns elect trustees or aldermen. Your local government may be different from Eric's, depending on where you live.

No matter how your local government is organized, though, running for office is going to be very much the same from one part of the country to another. It means having people sign petitions, putting up yard signs, going to meetings, and going door-to-door, talking to people in the community.

You don't need any special training in politics to run for local office. You can be a nurse, an accountant, an engineer, a farmer, or a college student. The next candidate in your hometown might be your teacher, your dentist, the clerk at the grocery store, or your neighbor. Or, in a few years, it might even be you.